FNWF
2023
SHORT
STORY
AWARD
WINNERS

GREATER
PACIFIC

Paperback ISBN: 978-0-6459322-0-1

First Published in 2023 by

First Nations Writers Festival International Limited T/as First Nations Publishers

A Registered Charity (ABN 79 655 932 979)

2/53 Junction St, Nowra NSW 2540, Australia

Phone: +61 491 851 353

Email: firstnationswritersfestival@gmail.com

Web: www.firstnationswritersfestival.org

FB: www.facebook.com/firstnationswritersfestival.com

Cover Design: Tim Axton

Typeset: Busybird Publishing

Printed and bound in Australia by IngramSpark

Line Edited: Anna Borzi AM 2023

Dedicated to all the first nation storytellers in the world.

Your stories create our history, our country, our customs, our community and future.

Our hopes, our dreams, our forever after.

Thank you.

Contents

Euralia Paine

of Papua New Guinea

THE JUDGES

Do cultures really clash? What is the norm in one culture? Aren't the ultimate goals the same in each? Is it the consequences of shifting lives that give rise to the clash, the problems? These difficult questions are asked by Euralia Paine in her compelling story THE PROMISE.

A FNWF2023 SHORT STORY AWARD was given to Euralia Paine of PNG by the Judges for this intellectual challenge in her story. Ancient cultures tested and proven over thousands of years for resilience; and recent events challenging those cultures. Are they able to find a common path forward. Is there an answer? A solution? Does someone pay a price?

The Greater Pacific stories have the best stories because these intellectual challenges remain and continue.

We write our country into being, and this story will contribute. Thank you for this incredible challenge.

Ms Paine said of her award, "I am humbled". So is FNWF2023. Thank you.

THE PROMISE

Euralia Paine

O n and off…on and off…like a flickering light. Katani goes into semi-consciousness and back. She lies face down on a pandanus mat, her head resting on a pillow. A coconut shell bowl of thick charcoal and water mixture sits beside her. Two women hold her hands down by her sides. A sharp citrus thorn taps rhythmically into the soft flesh of the back of her thigh. The small implement that hammers the thorn into her thigh sends her in and out of pangs of pain. Blood mingles with charcoal and trickles down her leg. The women massage her back and soothe her, preventing her from catching a glimpse of her own blood bleeding into charcoal. They gently rub freshly cut ginger stalk onto her skin to sanitise the wound and wipe away blood and charcoal.

Katani has reached puberty. Her aunties are tattooing her thighs to welcome her into womanhood.

The tattoo lines are as wide as the thick charcoal twig that repeatedly outlines her.

The thorn digs deep into her flesh to accentuate the lines.

Her grandmother Bua had told her, "These are the lines of your tribe, the markings of your ancestry, your lineage, your identity. Wear them proudly." She was reminded again as the tattoo continued.

"You are the steward of our traditional knowledge. The lines on your body are in sync with the lines on the *tapa* (mulberry bark) cloth you wear to protect your modesty. Just as your body, mind and spirit should be aligned to protect your tribal knowledge and values."

She had thought it pathetic that she was going to wear the family atlas on her body for the rest of her life. Was this a life sentence? Is this what I deserve as a female child?

Her mother had had it done. Her grandmother and her aunties too. Now it's her turn.

Her face twists in pain as she grimaces.

"If this is what womanhood feels like, I really don't want to go there," she mutters under her breath.

Katani was caught unaware. The stain was on the back of her blue dress with white frangipani flower. She had been sitting in the front pew with her mother in the women's section of the church. Right smack bang on the white frangipani was the red stain.

"God. Why now," thought her mother as she shielded her and took her home.

After that she had been put away for a month.

Her family had kept her in her room as it was her first menstruation. She was fed the best meals. Taro, bananas, and sago, served with the best fish and tu-lip (green leaves from a tree) cooked in coconut cream. She was only allowed to come out of the house after dark. No chores to do. No contact with friends.

Katani is the middle child. She has an older sister and a younger brother. She is slight and slender with quite fair skin. Her face is as oval as an avocado fruit and her eyes twinkle like stars on a moonlit night. People stop and stare when she is going to and from church with her mother. Others greet her just so she can raise her face for them to catch a glimpse. She is as industrious as she is beautiful. She is known for her *pasin* (good manners and good character).

Her ways are the ways of tribal nobility. She knows how to be respectful and treat her elders well. She is generous with her time and what she has, she freely shares. She was raised well in a household that was proud of its heritage, its lineage and its status as warriors and landowners.

Tattooing of a young woman's body after her first menstruation, takes on an added meaning. It is not just a sign of accepting a girl into womanhood, but also an initiation ritual that announces to the community that a granddaughter, a daughter or a niece is ready for marriage. The tradition makes permanent, the markings and patterns of a tribe on her body.

The tattoos are usually done by the girl's grandmothers or aunts. The ritual is a bonding session for the women who take turns to tattoo their young relative over several days. This is also an opportunity to advise and provide encouragement to the young woman so she can learn the ways of the tribe and her roles and responsibilities as a wife.

Firstly, wet charcoal is used to make the outline of the design or pattern on the body. A sharp thorn from a citrus plant is used as a needle. A twig is used as an implement to hammer the thorn into the skin. The thorn is pressed down over and over to make the puncture several times whilst the black charcoal and water is applied to redo the outlines.

The tattooist follows the design, adding more black mixture as she goes along, allowing it to enter the wound where the skin has been punctured. Freshly cut stalk of a wild ginger plant is used as lint to soak up excess blood. The ginger stalk is also used to buffer the pressure from the citrus thorn and the skin. The sap from the ginger stalk has medicinal qualities which should help to prevent infections and heal.

As gory as it may sound, the black charcoal mixed with blood in the flesh gives the forest green coloured tattoo on the skin afterwards. The whole procedure is done with great care and artistry and the finished look is regarded as a sign of beauty.

Katani was not allowed to wash her tattooed area for a month. She used coconut oil to massage and medicate the skin to heal well. The coconut oil is also an enhancer which brings out the tattoo designs. Sometimes Katani's aunt would reinforce the tattoo pattern on her thigh to make the design thicker and more distinct. The fairer the complexion of a young woman, the more outstanding the tattoos.

Katani's tattoos are very similar to the designs found on the *tapa* cloth that she wears at ceremonies. In Katani's society, the making of *tapa* cloth and its designs, and tattoos, are the domain of women. Women are the custodians of this intellectual property.

As was the case with girls, Katani was a late starter at school. She wanted to accomplish so much in life. Her teacher recognized her potential and encouraged her, even allowed her to repeat classes. She stayed away only because she did not know how to protect herself from the bleeding.

She was ashamed. She could not understand why she was bleeding every month. No one explained. It was taboo to talk about it. Her older sister had stopped going to school altogether because of it.

One day Katani decided to ask her grandma Bua for advice.

"Bubu (grandma), is there a fruit or a leaf that I could eat to stop the monthly bleeding?" The least Bubu could do was give her a helpful tip!

Bubu inhaled long on her tobacco and blew thick smoke in Katani's face.

"When it stops, you could be expecting....and we do not want that now, do weee?"

There was nothing to stop the painful cramps. There was nothing she could wear to stop the blood running down her legs. At school there was no separate toilet to go to.

Boys were always around, and she was embarrassed.

She asked her mother why....why...only to be yelled at that it was a female thing! It was something that could not be discussed with anyone, not even with her friends.

Is this another curse for being a female child, she wondered.

One day her aunty told Katani; "You are ready now my dear. Step into that ocean!" She had walked out into the sea feeling relieved, washing her thighs with salt water to reveal a distinct beautiful design running down the back of her pale thighs.

What a sight to behold! Bido's family had had their eyes on her since she 'came out of the house'.

One promise made all those years ago held on. Katani was chosen for Bido. The only son to a chief's first wife and most importantly, an heir. Bido's family is from a neighbouring household. His father, a well-known chief who owns a couple of businesses including a boat which operates along the coast to transport passengers and cargo.

It took a while, but Katani successfully completed her primary school. Sheer determination by her brother and her seemed

8

to have paid off. They would paddle their canoe to cross the bay to school every morning and return home. Sometimes, the challenges were too enormous. At a rural school such as theirs, there was a high turnover of teachers. Or, teachers would not be available for the start of the school year. There was also the lack of proper learning materials and resources.

It was such a jubilant time for the family when she got a place at high school. Her mother had hugged her tightly and cried tears of joy.

"A job will be your goal from now on. Focus on your studies. Work hard. Do not follow idle friends. Do not follow boys"; her mother stressed again and again as she busied herself preparing a nice meal to celebrate. "Always go to church on Sundays like we do here at home. Never forget to pray. God is good and He will take care of you".

Her father paced up and down the beach in front of their home wondering how far she would go in her education and whether it was wise to keep the 'promise'.

A promise made to the most powerful man in the community was just as good as it being set in stone. There was no turning back. He did not deem it wise for his daughter to fly out from under his wings. From high school Katani would have choices, opportunities and he knew her potential. She could go far, very far. Deep down he did not want to stop her. He was proud as plum of her achievement.

He reminisced of the time when she was about eight years old and had fallen and broken her ankle. He had taken her to the health center and stayed with her for almost a month while she was getting treatment. He had slept on the floor beside her bed.

Such precious memories…like those days too, when she would follow him to the garden. She would carry her little *bilum* (string bag) on her head and run to catch up with him. On the way back, she would collect shells to place in the *bilum*, even though it was already full to the brim with banana passion fruit.

His wish was always that she would get a nice job as a nurse or a teacher and return home to the local station to serve her people and look after him and her mother. Now it seemed like his dream would be a reality, he smiled to himself.

On the eve of her departure, Katani's parents sat her down for a chat. Her father explained the importance of keeping a promise in their society.

"It is about our value of integrity, standing by what we say we will do. It is about our tribal obligation to others in our community and the need to strengthen our relationships. We depend on each other in this environment. We stand by what we say to someone, especially if he is a respected leader," he said.

He then went on to explain that she had been promised to marry Bido. She was not surprised as she had been groomed by her mother and aunties to assist his family during feasts or when his mother had requested her help.

Her father had added; "But I want you to know I will support you and ensure you get the best education to have a good future."

Katani was confused. The door to a bigger, wider world had now opened.

Going to high school, meant going to college after that. And who knows….what else! One thing was for sure. She was determined to get out and make a life in a world of opportunities.

And she did. Katani and Bido began their relationship when she attended a teacher's college in the town where he worked. He had pursued her because of his family obligations. She had a vague memory of him from the village, but he seemed flashy in town. He worked for a mining company and enjoyed the trappings of success. In the beginning he was pleasant and generous, and she found his tall dark looks appealing.

Bearing a son, an heir to Bido, had made her all the more attractive to his family.

They then began discussions with Katani's family to formalise the marriage with a bride price ceremony.

Male voices in a hut:

~

First voice: *"K30, 000...that is the cash amount we should expect from Matoro, Bido's uncle. Don't forget, his oldest daughter is married to a foreigner, Australian or something."*

Second voice: *"I should have taken my chance when I was with her under the galip tree. Never mind, she could be useful now," he laughs.*

First voice: *"You know what, we should ask for a cow and a nice boat too." Second Voice: "Why not? Katani has the potential to complete a Diploma. She already has a son from Bido. She is an attractive young woman. And she is still able to bear more children."*

First Voice: *"Unlike my other cousins, she is very virtuous. To be honest I wish she found someone nicer but...Bido is able to pay big bucks; working with that mining company and all."*

Second Voice: *"Yeah...you are not wrong there. Lots of people are expecting big things at the bride price ceremony! I mean like, seriously Big Things!"*

Kutani's best friend and cousin Kora had warned her; "He is not husband material. Look at him. He thinks the sun shines out of his - you- know-what." The girls had laughed then.

From what she had heard, Bido was a 'player'. He thrived on his family's good standing in the community and his father's status to take what he pleased from the field. After all, he was the only son from the first wife of his father; a much adored and treasured child of his parents.

"Where have you been?" Katani yelled at Bido while opening the door. It was late at night. "Bloody powerless PPL (PNG Power Limited). Another blackout again", he swore under his breath. In the dark he had fumbled at the door for half an hour.

He stunk as a skunk.

And to Takira he yelled, "There you go again. Just like a stuck record."

"Why don't you just le..ee..ave if you don't like it here. This is my place, and I can do whatever I like."

Katani recoiled as she remembered that Bido was the reason, she had not completed her studies. She had her sights on being a teacher. She had received her Certificate from college. What she really wanted was a Diploma but that did not happen. She had fallen pregnant, withdrawn from college and moved in with him.

Her life with Bido in the past year had not been easy. His job as an engineer for a gold mine meant he spent 15 days on site and 14 days off site.

His time with his family became infrequent as he spent more time at bars and night clubs with his mates. When he arrived home late, fights would ensue and Katani would take her son and seek refuge in Kora's place across town. This abuse was taking its toll emotionally, but Katani had difficulty leaving Bido and the comforts of a home he provided for her and their son.

The bride price could be the glue to secure her relationship with Bido. It could make him stable. However, she feared his philandering ways would continue. She was concerned that he would use the bride price to threaten her family to prevent her from leaving an unhappy marriage.

Katani is torn between her obligations to her family, their expectations, and her own happiness. Living with Bido drained her emotionally. Yet she didn't want to disobey and disappoint her parents. They meant the world to her. They had sacrificed a lot for her.

They brought her up as devout Christian with ethical values. She was groomed and coached in the tribal ways. Deep down she understood that the bride price ceremony could benefit a lot of people including her family, her son and her.

Katani and Kora had just attended church. They were sipping tea and chatting under a tree. It was nice and peaceful when Bido was away on site.

"You know my family is expecting to benefit from your bride pride," Kora says to Katani. "We are the recipients and from the initial figures being discussed, we could be getting a lot. I hear Bido's family working around the country will be donating cash and goods.

"They all owe Bido's father one thing or another. Being a 'big man', he did so much for people and now they feel obliged to contribute to your bride price. Remember Rara, from the house up on the hill with the beautiful flower garden? Well, she is going to be cooking and delivering 40 dishes of food…40 dishes!! Can you believe that?"

Katani is taken aback. She is embarrassed by all the talk that has been going on about her bride price ceremony.

"To tell you the truth Kora, I am scared", Katani says pensively. "I understand that Bido is the best person to take care of all our family needs, including my parents. But you know what he's like. I am totally and utterly drained, emotionally, and physically. I don't know whether I can go on."

Kora is shocked at Katani's honesty and vulnerability. But not surprised. She has provided refuge for Katani and her son so many times.

"This is not about you, Katani!" Kora says firmly. "Bride price has never been about the girl. You know that. It's about Bido's father's influence, wealth and 'bigmanship'. Even Bido does not have a say in this. That's the sort of society we are born into." "Yeah…yeah," Katani replies resigned. "Every time I look around, I think I can see vultures swooping down."

"Come off it Katani! You are the most beautiful girl in our area. Bido's family knows that and they want to show their appreciation. I hear it is going to be the biggest most impressive bride price ceremony ever held."

Katani had not seen her parents in over two years. They seemed older and smaller in stature. Just a couple of years yet it had taken away so much. She felt tears sting her eyes at her impending loss. It pained her to see her father frail with a clumsy gait. Her mother was stronger but unable to do the normal chores well, she noticed. For several months her family had been preparing for the bride price ceremony. Her relatives from far and near had gathered.

Hugging her close and looking into her eyes Katani's mother told her, "This is it my dear. Bido has the means to make many people happy.

He can pay big - in cash, and goods. Perhaps an outboard motor with a banana boat, to boost your father's status. Anything..to boost that pride that we so need in our family..at least to take away the shame and disappointment you caused by falling pregnant and not finishing college."

Katani felt the sting and squirmed. Her mother was like that. She had a way of saying it like it was. She was known as 'bikmaus' (big-mouth) in the village. At least, the joy of village gatherings was something to look forward to.

Katani was going to catch up with all her cousins, aunties and uncles. She had not seen them in a couple of years and there would be many many stories to share. Maybe long into the night, on the beach in the moonlight, as she fondly remembered.

Many people are invited to attend and plans for a bride price ceremony can take months or even up to a year. During this time garden produce is grown to prepare for the event. Livestock is raised. Pigs penned and fattened. Poultry fenced and fed well. Fishermen are messaged to get their products ready. Funds are collected and saved. Extended families are requested to donate towards the ceremony in return for future favours they may require. Customary obligation is the rule of engagement. This means that families are obliged to contribute towards a bride price ceremony because they may need assistance in future.

"Have you seen the size of the kina and toea shells (traditional currency)? My goodness!"

Katani's younger sister Mandara is lying on a mat on the veranda speaking to no one in particular.

"His (rolling her eyes about Bido) family was cleaning out the cobwebs when I walked by their house. And the poles... there must be 10 of them! Enough to carry thousands and thousands of Kina notes (currency)."

Her mother looked up from the claypot which was full to the brim with food. She was cooking Katani's favourite food – sago with tu-lip leaves and smoked fish in coconut cream. "Go on, Mandara."

Mandara sat up and continued, giving her mother the side eye.

"I think they are show-offs! I bet you they are going to go all out to display their wealth without shame." She jumped off the veranda and left the house before her mother could say anything.

The bride's family is the recipient of most of the valuable items such as traditional currency or shell money; mainly to compensate her family for her upbringing. The groom's family receives the lesser amount of goods and currency from the bride's family as a sign of appreciation and to forge relationships.

"It's true, isn't it mother?" Katani was barking a statement more than anything else.

"In recent times, bride price ceremonies have taken on a new meaning. It's not like before...during your time. This tradition has become a competition among the well to-do families who try to outdo each other in their payments to the bride's family. Bride price ceremonies have become opportunities for men in our patriarchal society to seek status and reputation by showing off their wealth."

It wasn't a conversation her mother wanted to take part in. She could not remember her husband's family arranging a bride price ceremony for her. Deep down she felt she was not valued. But this was a different day and age. And it was not too late for some sort of redemption.

She replied while serving the sago pudding into a bowl. "Seize this opportunity with both hands; however it comes to you Katani. Do not shun it. Regard it as a blessing. Each contribution made is taken note of and accounted for."

"During a Thank you ceremony afterwards money, goods and food are distributed to those who have donated to the bride price ceremony. The more a family member contributes towards a bride price ceremony, the more that family will receive during the distribution of the spoils of bride price. The extended family network within our social structure is such that there are many donors and many recipients. Consequently, the more money a well-to-do family pays in bride price, the more influence this family will gain."

Her mother looked up at her: "At the end of the day, it's about establishing new bonds and strengthening old ones."

Katani had heard this cliché over and over recently and it was beginning to tire her. She swallowed a big spoonful of sago with relish. It was delicious. Her mother was the best cook she had ever known.

Dusk was here. The sun was beginning to disappear quickly through the coconut palms. It was always beautiful at this time. Sometimes the sky would be candy pink tinged with hues of brown. Other times the sky would light up in different shades of burnt orange. This time the sky was lemon yellow with black clouds as the sun slowly set between the coconut palms.

The crickets and cicadas came out and so did the women and men, and girls and boys. Merriment was about to begin. The melodies from the string band and gospel singing would soon ring through the night. It would be the sound of joy.

Swish..Swish of the *tapa* cloth, as the girls and women swing and sway in unison. Adorned in coconut shell armbands and scented leaves, their coconut-oiled bodies glisten in the moonlight. The sound of their sweet song accompanied by the rattles, float through the cool night air. They are dancing the *kere* (a dance performed by women only) which calls out to young men to join the maidens on the beach for a playful evening.

It is a dance Katani learnt as a schoolgirl. It is through this dance that she was taught the art of wearing her traditional *bilas* (dress). She fondly remembered her mother showing her how to put on a *tapa* cloth properly with a woven cane belt. The shell armbands, the heir loom shell necklaces, and a beautiful headdress would finish the look.

"It is in the way a girl moves, in her grace, her poise and mannerisms that her beauty really shines," she was told.

The stage is set for everything that she had been taught to be displayed with pride. The men will take their places according to the community and tribal hierarchy. Over betelnut chewing sessions and cheerful banter, they will beat the *kundu* and sing the chants in their *haus-win*.

Their culture is steeped in stringent protocols, values, and practices. It is passed down through generations in the form of storytelling and fables. It is marked by motifs on *tapa* cloth and tattoos, and in their traditional dress.

It is their proud heritage. It defines where they came from, their ancestry and their place in the ever-changing society. It is sacred and is a moral compass to guide their journey through life. They strive to protect their tribal intellectual property from being used indiscriminately, by others with no regard and respect, for the owners.

Katani was sitting in the *haus-win* (a shelter on stilts with no walls) with her parents. A black kettle over the fire underneath was a permanent fixture. But the *haus-win* she knew as a little girl, had been pulled down and rebuilt several times over the years. She had wonderful memories of the place. She remembered sitting and waiting for her father to open a *kulau* (young coconut) for her to drink. She envisioned her grandma Bua drawing long on her tobacco and then exhaling rings of smoke. She wished she could transport herself back to that time.

This was supposed to be her moment. A time when she would feel valued, that her worth would be reassured and defined. A time to be happy. But her heart was heavy. An emptiness had crept into the pit of her stomach. She felt a deep sense of loss and abandonment.

Katani is the first to speak: "I don't want to go through with this....this ceremony".

"I am sick of listening to everyone talking about what they can get out of it and how much. I am not a piece of pig that you can put a price on at the market. I have made up my mind. My son and I's happiness comes first."

Before she completes her sentence, her mother cuts in shouting angrily; "Who do you think you are? What happiness? Do you know the happiness your father and I have sacrificed for you? After all the things we have done for you, you treat us like this! You are an embarrassment. Ungrateful and disrespectful. I didn't raise you to be disobedient" She almost slaps Katani but stops and marches off fuming.

She turns back and yells at Katani.

"You can take your things and leave now; leave this house, leave this village. We don't ever want to see you again."

"Fine!" Katani shouts back at her mother.

She goes to the family house and packs hurriedly. She picks up her son sleeping peacefully in a *bilum* on the veranda. She calls her sister Mandara to carry him while she packs her bag to leave.

When Katani looks back, her father is still sitting on the mat, tears trickling down his face.

"Don't leave me like this," he pleads. "All I ever wanted was for you to get an education like I never got, have a job and make money like I never made. I wanted you to be independent yes…but I also wanted you to find a man who would take care and love you like I do."

Katani stops in her tracks, puts her bag down and looks around to see if her mother is around. Tears are streaming down her face.

Her father continues; "I suggest you go to Aunty Genda's place at the end of the village. That is a safe house. As you know she is Bido's father's archrival. Tell her I have sent you.

She will keep you until dark and the sea is calm. She has a canoe under dried coconut fronds safely tucked away at the beach that you and Mandara can use."

"I am not going to let you take my grandson away for good. I do not have much time left in this old body. Go quickly now. Do as I say. I will see you later tonight. Mandara, come and lead your sister through the back road."

Katani's father is unwell and getting good medical care would be the best way she could ever repay him. She will go to the station where she can get a signal on her cellphone. Then contact Kora in town.

Arnold Mundua

of Papua New Guinea

Stories create the culture and the country; the history and the future. So that when you write a story – you literally write the country into being.

A doyen of PNG literature is Arnold Mundua. Writing and published for a long time, he is an Elder of our Greater Pacific Literature. And his wonderful story has received an Award: AN UNEXPECTED INCIDENT AND I WAS MARRIED AGAIN.

Just the title makes you happy.

The Judges said of his Short Story Award FNWF2023 "Such warmth, such audacity, and humour, he takes you with him through the great losses and great joys of life. The unexpected that everyone in the world experiences so that this story could be you, wherever you are."

It is an honour for FNWF that such prominent Literary Elders are trusting us with stories.

AN UNEXPECTED INCIDENT AND I WAS MARRIED AGAIN

Arnold Mundua

It is often rare to find a Simbu man of my age to remain a widower for many years without the slightest hint of interest in women again, and perhaps children too after the true love had passed on. But I was different. I had promised and strictly maintained the pledge I made to my late Kauna over her grave and remained forever devoted to her by not getting married again. It was a promise I made after we had laid her to rest in our community cemetery, for I had considered no other woman on the planet equivalent to my late Kauna.

It was well over ten years ago that I made the promise and at forty I still kept the promise with diligence, respect and above all, my deep love for her even though she was not around. I avoided women, and sometimes girls too, who either had a crush on me or just wanted to flirt with me.

My behaviour raised a lot of questions in the minds of my friends and clansmen in Gowe, and even my parents who were in their late sixties. Perhaps I was too loyal to the promise I made, but many did not agree with the bachelor status I maintained for too long. They openly admitted that it doesn't look too good to see me as a widower for such an extended period of time. "You need a wife…and have kids", they said, "Kids are important". Yes, I agree, kids are important. But again, for some reason I turned them down, and occasionally refused to listen or communicate with anyone who wanted to discuss women with me.

It was the same down at Womatne. Occasionally, my uncles down the valley, who were now my only contacts left after grandfather passed away, sent word to find out if I had already found a new partner yet. They indicated through messengers that a couple of young pretty widows of my age were available for me to travel down and choose, if I had not hooked up with anyone yet. But I equally turned them down too, even refusing to visit them as I often did when grandfather was alive.

I could not understand why I behaved unhelpfully like that. But I should admit that I was either too stubborn to open up to other women, or that I was too lazy to get married and take up the role of a husband again. The latter seemed reasonable because all married men in Upper Simbu have a family to look after and worked twice as hard with added responsibilities than the bachelors. They dig and fence in new plots for the wife to plant. They build homes to house the wife, kids and the domesticated animals who share the same hamlet. They cart in firewood, sufficient to last for a week on a weekly basis for the wife to cook and keep the house warm. After my experiences with late Kauna, I decided to avoid these onerous tasks by not getting married again. And I felt comfortable as a bachelor.

But fate had its own plans for me. One day, some moons after the tenth anniversary of Kauna's death, Baglau Tenge, a young clansman fell ill. Baglau lived with his family downstream along the banks of the pristine Gowe. The news reached me and others from someone who'd come from the South. "He just fell ill and is in a bad state", said the messenger. And when we asked for Baglau's condition, he replied, "Really bad! The wife and kids are keeping a close watch".

Baglau and I were of about the same age. We grew up together in Gowe. As kids, whenever I was not down at Womatne with grandfather, we'd shared many happy moments together. With our little bows and arrows, we'd gone hunting for birds and marsupials in the forest. We played together with other kids and enjoyed just about everything that was available to the Upper Simbu kids of that time. In our teens we went through the initiation rites of *kua-ombuno* together. And off course, after our initiation into manhood we were ready for courtship with girls. There, under the cover of darkness, we'd formed a two-men team and roamed the valley for *ambai-kaugo* courtships, bombarding girl's homes with songs, or *kaugo-giglange*, that not many Upper Simbu males of our age could manage and equal our feats. Because our songs were original, ancient and entertaining that sent many girls and their mothers into a frenzy, compelling them to beg us to come back for more sessions with their daughters.

Our *kaugo-gilanges* were exotic and authentically ancient because we got them off directly from our mothers. Our mums were survivors of an ancient era and had scores of ancient songs shelved away in their memories. They had sung them with our fathers, and other courtship partners before the European contact. In the evenings before we went out to the girls' homes, they would teach us all the songs they had known and sung during their hey days. We would select an evening for time with my mother, to take out what she got in her archives and the next evening we would visit Baglau's mum for the same. In this way we accumulated a long list of songs. And when we released these numbers out in the girl's homes, they sounded new and exotic. They'd touch the hearts of many girl's mothers who'd kept the fires burning all night. And we'd amass praise and compliments at the end of every song. And to bag praises, compliments and requests from girls' mothers was a beauty, because we have literally conquered their hearts. Such praises and requests essentially gave Baglau and I, the advantage and freedom to enter homes and court with some of the prettiest girls in the valley and we felt superior. Without doubt we were regarded as the champion male team during those wonderful years.

But the teen life did not last forever. When the time came for us to choose our brides, Baglau chose his courtship partner Klara, a Denglagu lasso from the other side of the Gowe range, while I went for my childhood sweetheart at Womatne, the late Kauna. Marital life separated us. But as clansmen our bond and cultural roots were intact and we remained at close contact, supporting each other whenever needs arose, addressing each other as *yagl-kuna*, or 'my pal' whenever we crossed paths.

Unfortunately, it was not smooth sailing for me. I lost my Kauna during her first childbirth, and thereafter lived a widower, or *yagl werai*, as we call it in Upper Simbu. Baglau, on the other hand, lived and maintained a perfect marriage life with Klara and both produced two beautiful girls; Kaugo, aged six and Moro aged three years. The family settled peacefully some two hundred miles downstream along the banks of the Gowe river, where I sometimes visited them whenever I was passed through their territory. So, that morning I felt uneasy when news reached my ears that *yagl-kuna* was down.

At first I took Baglau's illness lightly, presuming it to be a common cold or fever that could be treated by the nuns at the Mission station clinic. But when later reports indicated that he was in a fragile state, I decided to pay him a visit. Two other male colleagues, Yokond and Mokene decided to accompany me too. And at about eight in the morning we headed downstream towards Baglau's house. We discussed Baglau's illness along the way, literally guessing on the possible causes. We also discussed the possible medications. "Goglau-nagle should have come along with us", Mokene said. And it was here that we realized something that we failed in our trip. Mokene was right, because Goglau-nagle was a renowned medicine man, a practitioner popularly known as *kumo-giai yagl* in the valley. He was frequently hired out to heal the sick on many occasions and his healing successes were unmatched by any other rival practitioner in the valley.

I witnessed Goglau-nagle performing his practice on two occasions. The first was not so convincing. He gave only water to the patient after whispering some indecipherable formulas into the cup. But in the second healing, he sat opposite his patient and demanded him to expose the affected part of his body to him. The patient pointed to an area around his tummy. Reaching into his medicine bag, Goglau-nagile took out a roll of tobacco. Placing the rolled tobacco between his lips, he lit the other end and puffed in, amassing thick clouds of smoke in his mouth. Moving closer to the sick man with his ballooned cheeks, he let out the smoke. He blew directly onto the affected area, gently rubbing and massaging the sick spot, as mumbled some indecipherable formulas. He continued in this way for sometimes.

Then putting away the tobacco, Goglau-nagile leaned forward. To our surprise he placed his mouth over the affected area. With both hands arranged flat on opposite side of the affected spot, he gently pressed, as if to feel something under the skin. Then slowly Goglau-nagle moved his pressing hands towards the spot where he'd placed his mouth. Suddenly, he started to suck vigorously on the affected spot, with his hands still pressing, as if to eject something out from under the skin into his mouth. After a while of gentle struggle with his mouth, he pulled back leaving the patient's skin wet all over. His mouth was seemingly full and tightly closed. Then moving his rustic and dishevelled frame over to a bed of leaves arranged beside him, he leaned forward and let out the contents in his mouth. To our amazement a host of unidentified objects coated with saliva landed on the leaves.

"There it is", said the medicine man, as he gasped for air. I starred in wonder, as I tried to figure out how the foreign objects made their way in, and then out again through the medicine man's mouth without leaving any traces of cuts or damages on the patient's skin. It was a mystery and everyone who witnessed were held spellbound. Unfortunately, it was part of Goglau-nagle's healing practice and he was never to disclose his skill.

"What is that?" someone finally asked, and the medicine man replied, "Let's find out". And using a little stick that was passed to him, Goglau-naigle toyed around with the unidentified objects, gently removing the thick saliva coatings and finally exposed a boar's molar tooth before us. "Someone wanted you dead", Goglau-nagle uttered, "He placed a boar's tooth in your abdomen to destroy you". We looked at each other, hardly daring to speak. "But we are lucky to take them out", the medicine man continued, "I'll give you water and you'll be fine", he assured his patient. Holding a cup of water before him, Goglau-nagle lit his tobacco again. He puffed thick clouds of smoke into the cup while mumbling yet another lot of indecipherable formulas. Seconds later he handed the cup to the patient. "Drink!" he ordered, and the sick man did as he was told. Surprisingly, the patient left his sick bed a few days later.

It was an incredible performance but that morning Goglau-nagle slipped off our minds and we regretted the oversight terribly, as we proceeded downstream.

We were less than a hundred yards from Baglau's house, when a sudden noise of wailing and keening filled the air. It resonated far and wide and was coming from Baglau's residence. For a while we stood frozen because in Simbu such peculiar sound could mean nothing less than death claiming someone's life. And with Baglau reportedly ill, we instantly knew something terrible must have happened to him. "He must have passed on", Mokene reluctantly voiced. None of us dared to speak. I was lost, not knowing what to say. Suddenly, I realized my *yagl-kuna*, was down, or did he? And we cannot be wasting any more time there. "Let's go and find out", I said, and we doubled our paces.

The wailing sounds also caught the attention of the neighbouring citizens, and those within reach scurried over to investigate. Baglau had died. Outside in the open we found Klara twisting and turning on the ground amidst uncontrollable tears. She was pulling on her hair to self-inflict physical pain over the loss of her husband. She lost her loved one and it was not strange to see her in such a state and behaviour.

Simbu women are notorious for over reacting in times of grief, especially over the death of a loved one. Klara could have chopped one of her ten fingers off in memory of her late husband. Past instances had witnessed widows jumping over cliffs or into fast flowing rivers to permanently end their grief. However, the good missionaries had condemned such acts, denouncing them as acts of paganism and the habits had died out. But emotions are often difficult to control sometimes, and Klara was under close watch as she mourned.

Everyone who entered could not spare a moment to express their grief and sadness of losing one of our prominent clansman, friend and citizen. Sounds of whining and keening erupted from all corners where a mourner entered. I stood firm at first, but as soon as my eyes caught sight of my *yagl-kuna's* motionless frame lying beside the fireplace---the spot where he'd been reportedly bedding when he went down---I broke down at the doorway. Like everyone else there, I held my head low between my two cupped hands, and as if two drain plugs were pulled out of my eyes, I let out litres of warm tears down my cheeks. Baglau was my childhood friend, clansman and *yagl-kuna*. When I reminisced on our past, not a drop was left in my eyes.

Baglau's death will attract a huge crowd of mourners from locations far and wide later in the day and in the coming days.

So, after regaining composure, a meeting was quickly held amongst those present. We discussed what to do next and immediately resolved to take Bagalu's body upstream to the central communal ground in Gowe, where the men's house and the clan's ceremonial ground were located.

We silenced the mourners and I announced the plan. We assigned a team to construct the stretcher. A second team was assigned to prepare Baglau's body for the long walk upstream, when the stretcher team would arrive. Mokene, Yokond and I stayed behind with the second team. We would oversee the cleaning and dressing of Baglau's body. But I purposely stayed back to take care of my *yagl-kuna's* body for the last time. A third team was sent to Gowe to alert everyone there and prepare the place to hold Baglau's body in state for the mourning.

When the two teams were gone we immediately went to work. But as we were cleaning and dressing Baglau's corpse, something unusual happened that raised many eyebrows and would later be the subject of a series of other extraordinary events in the coming days. As two men carefully lifted Baglau off his death bed, fresh blood suddenly oozed out of Baglau's nose. Noticing this strange incident, the two men quickly called me to witness the scene. It was abnormal for a corpse to bleed profusely when the heart had stopped many hours earlier. I quickly grabbed a cloth and wiped Baglau's face clean. But the blood flow seemed endless as Baglau's body was moved, turned and rolled around. "You have to stop this, *yagl-kuna*", I gently whispered into Baglau's ears, as I did the cleaning. And almost miraculously the blood flow stopped.

The stretcher team arrived. They had constructed the stretcher using bamboo strips woven around two poles. A blanket was quickly spread out over the stretcher, and Baglau's corpse was lifted onto the stretcher. He was laid out in a supine position with the knees in bent position to fit the stretcher. The blanket edges were then folded over and around Baglau's body, giving the corpse a good wrapping. Twines were used to fasten the corpse to the stretcher to keep it steady during the long walk.

When everything was set two young men stood at both ends of the stretcher, lifted Baglau off the ground and placing the ends of the poles over their shoulders, the long walk upstream began. Behind the stretcher-men were men, women and children that had gathered at Baglau's place. We reached Gowe in the amidst of heavy grieving and wailing. The third team had prepared everything for our arrival and we placed Baglau on a raised platform in the centre of the ceremonial ground for the public viewing and mourning.

The news of Baglau's demise fanned out to all corners of the valley. And as the day brightened up, mourners attended in multitudes; friends, relatives, in-laws and many more, all drenched in mud over their faces and bodies. It was the beginning, for in our society, our clan was in mourning until when the body was buried and we expected many more mourners in the coming days.

Baglau's maternal uncles were the Inaugls from the South. We expected them any moment but there was not a sign of them. Rumour reached Gowe that the Inaugl's were planning a group mourning and will arrive any moment. This was not strange, for it now became obvious that Baglau's uncles would attend in the conventional *kunda-dekwa* fashion. We knew what to expect in such situation and quickly alerted everyone to get the kids and the old to stay away from the mourning grounds when the Inaugls would arrive.

On the morning of the second day the Inaugls finally arrived. Drenched in thick black mud and armed with sticks, Baglau's uncles entered the Gowe grounds with aggression and hostility. They went on a full rampage, as if they were on a mission to annihilate us. There was outrage demonstrated with humiliations, beatings and property destructions. In Kuman, such mourning rampage is called, *kunda-dekwa-wigua*. It was pre-planned and was executed without mercy and show of respect to the other mourners.

They provoked, beat, kicked and punched every person in their way and destroyed every plant that grew in their path. Women were slapped. Men were kicked and punched. Food gardens behind the houses were destroyed. I took an unexpected punch from a mud drenched Inaugl. I did not remain to collect a second one. Several others followed me to avoid the same, leaving behind a few brave ones, as the humiliations took place.

We took the beatings and watched everything that took place without retaliation. This was part of our custom, the conventional way of all uncles to show their frustration, pain and grief over the loss of one of their off-shoots, or *imbo-sien-digua*, as we call it. They were sad at losing Baglau, especially when he was still in his peak moment.

When the Inaugls finally settled, they crowded around Baglau and viewed his body. There was weeping, keening and bawling, some pulling on their hair. After what seemed like an hour or more, they regrouped to one end of the ground and produced five porkers and K1000.00 cash as condolence payment to us. Such payments were forthcoming when they went on the rampage, and so, at the hour of dismissing the Inaugl's back to the South, we reciprocated by doubling their gifts. We gave K2000.00 cash and produced eight porkers as 'compensation' to settle their grief and anxiety over the demise of their descendant.

It was decided that Baglau would be interned on the fourth day. Usually, the burial of our dead takes place in the afternoons, with the grave digging and preparations of the burial grounds taking place in the morning. In Upper Simbu, a grave is never dug and left open till the following day, for it was widely believed that a fresh grave left open overnight will start 'calling' for more bodies to come in. Fearing more deaths all graves were dug and covered on the same day.

On the set day for Baglau's burial, grave diggers set out in the morning at six to prepare the grounds. Towards evening when the clock pointed to three, my *yagl-kuna* was finally lowered into his resting place, amidst crowds who held back nothing in their eyes for the last time. It was the same cemetery where my late Kauna and son were buried. As my *yagl-kuna* was lowered, I briefly glanced at Kauna's grave. The timber crucifix was no longer there. I recalled how she and our infant were lowered into the grave. A moment of pain swept through my inside as the images come and go in my mind. I looked away making sure not to look there again. My *yagl-kuna* was joining them now and they would be neighbours soon.

A week after the burial was the feast of *kugl-gaugl* to end the moments of mourning, keening and grieving. It is also known as *gamba-buko-diguwa*, where mourners cleanse themselves of the mud and clay over their faces and bodies. Garden crops were carted into Gowe, *mumu* leaves were readied and after a week of preparation, each household killed a porker that totalled well over twenty. Klara slaughtered two pigs with her parents-in-law. My parents clobbered one, and in an afternoon filled with crowds of friends, relatives, and distant mourners, the cooked pork was ready for distribution.

Feasts and gatherings of such magnitude do not go without speeches. And when everything was set, selected orators from the host team walked out and took their turns. The first speaker was Kaiglo. With an axe in his hand that symbolizes authority, he walked up and down the central arena in front of the dishes of cooked food and delivered his speech. When he retired the next speaker went in. There were about four speakers, and the last was our councillor, Nime Maglum.

Councillor Nime reviewed events of the past week. He acknowledged everyone who attended and shared the moment of grief with the Gowe community. He rattled on and then in his concluding statement he voiced the unexpected, saying; 'since Yaltep was Baglau's *yagl-kuna* (pal), and that he was a *yagl-werai* (widower), it was fitting for him to '*yagl kunamo embie werai kambe ninabuka* (...take possession of his pal's widow)'.

The Councillor's words caught me off-guard and I froze in the middle of the crowd. Such announcement was unusual in any mourning gatherings, or feasts held in honour of the dead. When I looked around several eyes turned towards my direction with smiles. The Councillor's speech ended, and he proudly walked away, perhaps a satisfied man, as if he had just delivered the most powerful speech of his lifetime.

For the moment the speech was indeed powerful, for it kept me motionless in the crowd. Baglau's passing would leave Klara on her own, and I never thought about it. She would obviously be up for grab by any male partner, and now Councillor Nime's speech appeared a test of time and challenge never once put before me in my life.

Already the widow's face was coming and going in my head. I took a furtive glance at Klara to assess her reaction as food distribution was underway. She was in a section occupied by her in-laws, and nothing seemed apparent on her face. She was obviously weak from the long moments of mourning but appeared unaffected from the Councillor's speech. She was content in her dishevelled appearance, as if she heard nothing from the Councillor.

I was the most affected. The challenge was something unusual after being ignorant of women for a long time and in all seriousness, Councillor Nime's proposition was already taking roots inside me. Klara was charming. She was pretty too and was an excellent choice for a wife. She had attributes similar to my late Kauna and I already felt a fire of love and desire glowing inside me. Equally, I felt excited too.

Reminiscing on the promises I made over Kauna's grave, it was different this time. Unlike the moments after her death, there was no longer any inclination to keep honouring the oaths, or the promises I made, for time had gradually eroded away the memories of her that were attached to me. She was now a mere shadow in the back of my mind. Perhaps Councillor Nime's speech created a miracle, and it was Klara who stood out in my mind.

Other provoking thoughts also boosted my craving for Klara. In our society where the patriarch system reins, I needed a son to be my heir after I am gone. I had none. There wasn't even a brother before or after me too, and my aging parents were very worried. And so, with this pressing matter also before me, I felt the attraction and urge towards Klara demanding and gaining momentum as the clock ticked. Klara also had two beautiful girls who would soon reach their teens.

They were sure to deliver any step-father, handsome bride-prices when they were married. So with all the advantages presenting themselves before me, I convinced myself that the time was right for me to take a bride again.

It is conventional for a widow to remain in her late husband's village until such time, when she was possessed by another man, and taken away to his village to marry her. Klara was still in her prime age. Mother of only two kids, I wouldn't be so sure what she has in mind about her future. But Simbu men are cunning. I knew there were other men eyeing her too, even before Baglau was put into the ground. And I must act fast before someone takes advantage of my ignorance.

Exactly a week after the mourning feast I made my first visit to Klara's house. I timed my arrival and got there towards dusk, when I knew Klara and her girls would be home. I had carried a log with me for firewood and the thumping noise at the doorway when I dropped the log alerted them of a visitor outside the house. With my axe I split the log into firewood sizes first. Then I entered the house. I was their family friend and the reception I got was welcoming. They greeted me ardently. Klara perhaps knew precisely why I was there, at this time of the hour. In Simbu we call such visit *ambu-werai-midigua*.

She has also heard Councillor's Nime's grand speech, and reacted with slight hesitation at first but remained content, perhaps not wanting to confuse her daughters. It was different with the girls. Both reached out to me with smiles, and behaved in manners least expected from kids who'd lost their loving dad recently. At this sight my heart melted. In that brief moment, I reached my decision to take the girls as my own children. After the silent but warm exchanges of pleasantries, I handed over my first parcel of gifts, comprising sugar, tea and rice.

Klara remained composed through the night. There was no hint of protest or disappointment. She, like any Kuman widow would do, accepted my gifts and prepared dinner. She cooked using the firewood that I'd brought along, and shelved the remaining woods up in the firewood rack above the fire place. I felt nervous and strange at first, for it was my first time to embark on such mission. And taking dinner with Klara and her girls in the absence of Baglau made me feel even more awkward. It was a new experience and I remained calm and allowed courage to build up, which it eventually did as the night wore on.

I left close to midnight, confidently assuring myself that I could now frequent Klara's house at any time. But Upper Simbu men are not blind, for they are sensitive and cunning when they hear of a widow living by herself. Usually, after the passing of a husband the race among men to take possession of the widow begins without a stop. And for Klara, I was not alone to visit her with my gifts. In spite of the fact, that I was publicly declared to take possession of Klara, there were other rival men interested in her too. I was not wrong, for I discovered that several men had visited her at odd hours behind my back with their gifts.

Like a teenager I felt hurt and jealous too, but it was Klara who'd make the final choice from the potential husband candidates visiting her. Strangely, I decided not to allow Klara to make that choice. I began to sense the danger of losing her if I was not smart enough and planned to make my visits more frequent instead.

Putting my plan into action I showed up in Klara's house on a daily basis, sometimes in the morning to spend time doing menial jobs for her, like patching a leaking roof, or digging up a small backyard plot for her to grow vegetables.

Once or twice a week, I'd deliberately excuse Klara and her girls for a tired day, and slept in their home. The whole plan worked brilliantly. Upon noticing my frequency in Klara's home, many male rivals ceased to visit her. Eventually, Klara was now mine.

There were widespread approvals amongst my friends and clan members when they learnt of my union with Klara. They encouraged me to take her to my house. My parents were happy too. Among them was Councillor Nime. He proudly boasted that it was his doing, that brought Klara and I together and congratulated me to the heavens.

One evening about the fourth month after my first visit, I asked her if she and the girls could permanently leave their home and come with me. Klara consented, and so one morning after carefully packing their scanty belongings we departed her late husband's residence forever and walked upstream to my Gowe home. There we moved into my parent's home. A week later, a light matrimonial feast was held, attended by parents and close relatives of my late *yagl-kuna* to formally recognize the matrimony and welcome Klara and her girls into their new home.

It was a special occasion for me after living a bachelor's life for a long time. But I also sense the dangers of the tribulations and curses from the dead that might befall on me for breaking the oaths and promises. And so, on the night after the feast, I decided it was fair to inform Baglau and Kauna about the situation, and maybe ask for their blessings too. While on my way to the men's house I visited the cemetery. Posing before Kauna's grave I mumbled my confessions, highlighting the latest twist of fate. I asked her to forgive me and support the decision I made. I emphasised the need to have a son to continue the family tree and since she was not around to oversee that I asked for her understanding and blessing. Then turning to Baglau's grave, I assured him that I had to do this because it was everyone's wish and asked for his support too. I also promised to look after his two girls, and that he shouldn't worry too much about them. I tried to think of anything else to blurt out, or that if I had missed something. But nothing popped up in my head.

Satisfied and certain that I had perfectly communicated with the spirits of the dead, and confident that I had bagged their approval and support, I took off at breakneck speed towards the *yagl-ingu*, occasionally turning back to check if anything like Baglau, or Kauna was following me. I was wet all over from the sweat that oozed out like running water from my body. There was nothing following me, or blocking my way in the front too. It was all my own imagination that had prompted me to run.

When I reached the nearest residential area, I ceased the running and continued with a walk. A hundred metres from the *yagl-ingu*, I dropped onto a boulder by the roadside. I did not want to arouse suspicion in a drenched state. Satisfied that the sweat all over me had disappeared, I stood up and slowly walked into the *yagl-ingu*. No one seemed bothered. I crawled onto my bed and stretched out for a peaceful rest. Recalling all my 'adventures' in the last four months, I tried to piece together everything. But it was too much. All I remembered was I had married my pal's wife and became a married man again before closing my eyes for the night.

Paulini Turagabeci

Of Fiji

"The arc of a young woman's life, from the cultures of the past to the present….what? Beautifully narrated, structurally balanced, multi layered, almost light in nature – until you sit back at the end and think. This is magnificent literature from the Greater Pacific. Congratulations."

TOBE

Paulini Turagabeci

'Saturday afternoon in the sweltering heat of December. My friends and I sat killing time at the bus stop of the Nabua housing projects, somewhere I wasn't supposed to be. Tina nudged me. I followed her gaze across the street and recognised Alumeci coming out of her block, holding her yellow *suluvakatoga* twisted in her hands. She paused to tuck the fabric around her waist and keep it from falling. Alumeci looked frail even from a distance.

Seini, her mother, a canteen lady at the Nabua Girl's school, held her teenage daughter around the waist as they descended the dusty, dank stairs toward a waiting taxi. The overcrowded urban housing projects in Nabua came to a standstill to watch and whisper. Someone called out, "What's going on?"

At the bottom of the stairs, Alumeci, pale and hunched over, could not take a further step.

A tattooed young man in a Marist 7's vest caught her before she collapsed. He lifted her into his arms much like they do in old Sky Pacific TNT movies I watched secretly on Saturday nights when my grandparents were asleep. Alumeci's *suluvakatoga* stretched taut against her thighs and buttocks, and the nature of the emergency revealed itself. Dark red spots appeared, mottling the yellow fabric like a strange butterfly spreading its wings.

Tina, Lo, and I passed around a packet of crushed chicken-flavoured Maggie noodles as we added our commentary to the scene that played out in front of us. The crunch of uncooked noodles in our mouths sounded irreverent considering the seriousness of Alumeci's ordeal.

"It's cos she drank a whole bottle of Nescafe in one sitting." Tina's loud whisper inferred conspiracy. "No milk. No sugar."

Lo, Tina's cousin shook her head, "*Segai*. She's a Seventh Day Adventist. The *Kavitu's* don't drink coffee."

Tina bristled. "I'm just repeating what I heard. Who cares about breaking a dietary rule anyway when you want to commit a bigger sin of *vakalutu.*"

I remained silent. It was hard to take sides between a mother and her unborn child. I uncoiled my *tobe*; the lock of hair tucked away into a ball near my right ear. It was a subconscious act - a compulsion when I was agitated, deep in thought, or working out a lie in my head.

"I wonder if it hurts as bad as it looks," I said.

The sight of blood made my stomach turn but I was mesmerised nonetheless, finding it hard to pull my gaze away.

Tina snickered. "Bet she wished she stayed a virgin."

I didn't miss the side-look Tina passed me as she said the

words. I stopped playing with my *tobe* immediately and slid them back behind my ear.

I stayed as long as I could to linger in the gossip. But soon, I hurried back home to Lot 5 Galu Lane before Grandma returned from choir practice.

I couldn't tell her about Alumeci. She forbade me to mingle with "*people whose only goal in life was to reproduce and live off of government handouts.*"

If she ever found out that I had sat and talked to the inhabitants of "*the great criminal incubator,*" her fifty-year-old arms were still strong enough to whip my twelve-year-old legs with the cut-off hosepipe she kept in her bedside drawer, next to her Bible. Grandma was never lost for contemptuous descriptions about the projects. I hated to admit it, but she wasn't all wrong. The projects were known for their fair share of brawls, glue sniffing, and drug deals.

We lived only three streets away from the Nabua housing projects. According to municipal zoning, we were still in the same jurisdiction. But Grandma did her utmost to belie the fact.

Our three-bedroom bungalow was barricaded by a white picket fence while our neighbours made do with wizened iron gates, rusting beneath peeling paint, or no gate at all.

Grandpa's twenty-year-old Toyota Corolla sat parked on our driveway; a driveway constantly plastered with white cement powder for a clean, decorative effect. The perimeter of our front yard boasted manicured rows of flowers that ran parallel to the fence. S*inu* and *senitoa* bushes primmed and proper. A pink phobia here and a white orchid there. At night, security lights lit the yard, and when I smelled the ethereal scent of *jiale* floating on a visiting wind, I thought I could live in that house forever and be quite content.

A frangipani tree grew crookedly on our bent grass lawn.

"I planted this tree and buried your mother's *vicovico* with it," said Grandma.

She never liked the wayward crookedness of the frangipani tree. But I loved it. It had more character than the struggling-to-live *Kavika* tree Grandma buried my umbilical cord with. Every year I wished in vain to finally taste the *Kavika's* white juicy fruit. And every year the stubborn tree refused to yield. Despite Grandma and Grandpa's threats at the *Kavika* tree to cut it down, they seemed to hold out hope that the new year would bring some fruit.

On the other hand, when the frangipani tree was in full bloom, it looked like pink stars with a yellow core had fallen from the sky and adorned the branches. I especially liked it when the flowers littered the ground. There was beauty in the mess. But Grandma detested the slightest debris on the lawn and I was wise to rake away evidence of nature's natural deterioration before Grandma needed to tell me.

For all her austerity, Grandma was sentimental. She kept a wooden chest of traditional family heirlooms in her bedroom. Once in a while, she'd take out her *masi* bridal gown, the fan she held during her wedding with her name woven across it, and the five large whale's teeth Grandpa gave her when he asked her to marry him.

"A woman who keeps herself until marriage is to be envied," she'd say. Sometimes her eyes took on a faraway look when she said, "My mother wore this *masi*. Sala was supposed to wear it too." She never said I would wear it someday. But if the line of succession should continue, it was my turn next.

Grandma's old family pictures as a newlywed and a new mother showed a happy young woman who couldn't keep a smile off her face. I often wondered where that woman went.

That night, I watched headlights play across my ceiling as I lay in bed—the scene from the projects replayed in my mind's eye.

For the umpteenth time, I wondered why my teenage mother, Sala, had me. Was it because she didn't know how to get rid of me?

Determined not to feel abandoned, I made myself believe that Sala had thrown me a lifeline by choosing to keep me. Although only long enough to leave me with my grandparents when I turned three.

Alumeci's unborn child would never experience playing in the sun or feel the gritty sand massage the soles of her feet. She'd never taste Rewa butter on breakfast crackers or cream buns from the Hot Bread Kitchen. She'd never sit under a broken garter during heavy rains or feel the thrill of running home with friends at the last trill of the school bell.

Then again, she would never suffer the rap of a wooden spoon on the tips of pinched fingers when you stained the front of your uniform with the dribblings of pink ice-block. Or the swish of the hosepipe across your behind because Grandma found you in the guava tree with friends at twilight. Or the disappointment when your crush likes your best friend, but you smile like it doesn't hurt inside.

In the morning, I thought I had slept under a leaking roof. My bed was damp, despite having left bed-wetting years ago. My soppy underwear clung to me with uncharacteristic stickiness. My dark sheets had a darker spot of wetness resembling the rippled edges of an oyster shell. I ran three fingers across it and brought it to my nose. It didn't particularly smell like anything. Only after, did I look at my fingers and notice the pale crimson of watery blood. If I had been stabbed, I felt no pain.

But I reluctantly made the connection. Wet sheets - wet underpants - red. Two years earlier, in class five, the popular girl in my class, Rosi, and a group of our peers watched as a class seven girl rushed to the restroom.

Rosi giggled. "She must be on her period."

The other girls giggled along with her and I joined in the laughter. Only to hide the truth that I hadn't a clue what or who a period was.

I went home and waited eagerly for Grandma to return from her job selling Fijian handicrafts to tourists. She rented a stall at the Handicraft centre along the Suva seawall. Her *buiniga* stood proud, unbungled by the day's labour. She smelled of Elizabeth Arden's Red Door when most grandmothers I knew smelled of *mokosoi* scented coconut oil or Kris perfumed cream at a dollar a bottle.

"Grandma, what's a period?"

I sat at the dining table, completing my social studies homework defining cultural integration, assimilation, and segregation.

Grandma's eyes nearly popped out of their deep-set sockets. She had been counting her day's earnings and dropped a tawny brown five-dollar bill on the kitchen floor. "Where did you hear that from? Did you have your period?" she asked in quick succession.

I shook my head, uncertain.

"I don't send you to school to talk about periods. Next thing you know, you will be talking about boys and then you…" Grandma froze mid-sentence.

I watched with muted concern as her face paled, then

flushed with cornered embarrassment. Then it quickly turned into anger.

She grabbed a nearby *taufale*, but I knew she had no intention of sweeping the room. Usually, when she intended to give me a hiding, she'd calmly retrieve the hosepipe from her drawer, then beckoned me with her hands tightly grasped around the two ends of the tube.

But before I knew it, Grandma had yanked me by the arm out of my chair and laid the *taufale's* wooden handle across my legs and buttocks.

Try as I might to contain my cries, the whole neighbourhood heard my screams of pain and entreaty for mercy.

We were still in a tangle of arms, legs, and *taufale* when Grandpa raced in from a neighbour's house where he had been sharing a baby mix of *yaqona* and recounting the coup of '87, the year of my birth.

"What's going on here? I thought there was a fire," he panted.

"Stay out of this, Eroni. Lavenia has been learning ungodly things at school and she must be punished."

Grandpa, never one to get in Grandma's way, gave me a sympathetic glance and returned to the neighbour.

I spent the rest of my days thinking that a period was something you did in secret. Then whisper in bashful mischief to a peer who navigated the shadowy halls of pre-teen and adolescence with you.

It wasn't much later, say three months after the beating, that I understood what a period was.

"When a girl gets her period, she sheds the inner lining of her uterus walls, and blood is discharged through the vagina," explained Mrs. Ulu in one of those class's boys weren't allowed in.

My curiosity was satiated, and while the terms Mrs. Ulu scratched on the blackboard were insightful, it was all rather anticlimactic. Nevertheless, I blocked out periods and every word associated with it like they were vulgar. All so I wouldn't rile Grandma up again.

I scurried to gather my sheet into a heap before I opened my bedroom door slowly, glanced left to right across our small hallway, then slipped out in search of an empty bucket. I threw my soiled bed sheet into the bucket and filled it with water. "What's that on your shorts?" Grandma had been inspecting her garden, and in her hands, she carried a small bouquet of flowers for the kitchen table as was her Sunday morning ritual.

The last time my heart leaped so high it almost lodged itself in my throat was when I had stolen a spoonful of milo and swallowed it underneath the kitchen table. I thought I had been well hidden. Grandma caught me out then as she did now. But this time, she was staring at something in plain sight and not what I was trying to hide.

I had been so preoccupied hiding the evidence on my sheet I was blind to the sizeable splotch of red gracing my cream-coloured sleeping shorts.

My lips quivered, and my eyes watered as if I was facing a sentence for my crimes.

Grandma's features softened before hardening again.

"You're having your period, silly girl. It's natural, and it's painless. Why are you crying?" Her non-violent reaction threw me off a little. Grandma wasn't the affectionate type. At least her love language wasn't touch. She kissed out of a sense of propriety - that's what *I-taukei* women did when they met. She kept a large face towel in her mat-woven purse to wipe away the scent of other women, their sweat, or the stray residue of saliva left on her after a close embrace. Grandma would nearer beat me to death than asphyxiate me with hugs.

Needless to say, there were no hugs or kisses for crossing the channel from girl to womanhood.

Instead, Grandma removed every meat she could find in the freezer; chicken, fish, and pork, then busied herself silently in the kitchen.

"Have your shower, ask grandpa for two dollars, then run to the shop. Buy a packet of pads."

The short walk was long, lonely and mortifying. I worked the word 'pads' on my lips unsure whether to say it like the gentle movements of a dying fish' mouth. Or the forceful spurt of one spitting out sand.

At the dark, shelf-congested corner shop, I gritted out the word hesitantly. I couldn't answer when the male shopkeeper asked which pad brand I wanted. Neither could I look him in the eyes when he suggested one that fit my budget. I only nodded and raced out of there as though exiting a house on fire.

Later that afternoon, Grandma took me to the *tatala's* home, within the compound of our Methodist church. She carried a basket of honeyed pork, chicken stew, and fish in *lolo* reverently in the crook of her arm. I walked behind her and played with the length of my *tobe*.

"*Talatala, na neitou goneyalewa sa goneyalewa*," announced Grandma in a proud tone she hadn't used on me earlier.

I often replayed that sentence as if it were some unsolvable maths equation: *Pastor, our young girl has become a young woman.*

But *Talatala* and his wife, *Radini Talatala* knew exactly what the phrase meant. They had a brood of seven children themselves, four of them girls.

I sank beneath the adult conversation traversing above my head, willing the heat to leave my face, but not quite conquering the discombobulation that a discharge from my private parts should earn such hoopla.

"Well, young lady, now that you have become a woman, you have the responsibility to protect the sanctity of your body," said the *Talatala*, among other things that made me squirm in the seat of my *sulu-i-ra*.

Radini Talatala knelt beside me and placed gentle hands on my shoulders as *Talatala* prepared to pray over me.

"God has wonderful plans for you, Tobe," she said. And everyone glanced at the lock of hair I had tucked back into a ball beside my ear.

Funny how monikers stick; *Leka* for a short person, *Maji* for kinky hair, and *Matadua* for my aunt with one eye. Mine came about as early as five years old when Grandma cut my hair short but left a lock of hair by my right ear. She sent a picture to Sala in America. It caused a big fight over our rotary dial phone.

"Why do you have to do that to her? They'll tease her at school." I heard Sala's voice even as I sat at the verandah pretending to play with my one legged doll.

"It's beautiful, and you should be here to do it," said Grandma just as angrily.

"No girl wears a *tobe* anymore. I didn't wear one. Girls don't even wear it until they hit puberty."

Grandma kept silent because she knew it was true. In the olden days, a mother began to groom her daughter's hair at around eleven or twelve years old. The hair was often shaved, leaving only a portion around the ears or the base of the head.

It was something special shared between mother and daughter.

Unfortunately, Sala only graced our presence with an infrequent letter or a short postcard on the rare days she could leave her job as a caregiver to the aged, and try out touristy things. Like cheese tasting on an organic farm in Oregon. She complained about expensive international calls on the rarer occasions she made them.

"You've changed," Sala accused. "Grown crazy."

Sala might have won the war of words, but Grandma won the battle of wills and I wore my tobe obediently. I didn't know it then, but my tobe was not a fashion statement. It was a symbol of my purity - virgin locks to be paraded in silent arrogance, shackled to me until a husband set me free.

Sixteen and I flirted with rebellion. Youths from the Nabua projects were having a *gunu sede* at their community hall for their volleyball team; fundraising around *yaqona*, dancing, jesting, and for some, horizontal play later.

Tina invited me. I accepted. Tina was not my best friend, but she was the closest I had to one outside school. Even though we both knew what I was, was more akin to a sidekick. Every superhero needs a sidekick to help make her look good, and every sidekick requires a superhero to aspire to become, even if only wishfully.

Grandma and Grandpa headed off to Namosi for an important weekend village meeting.

They wanted me to go but I stayed on the pretext of studying for a Geography test on Monday.

I stole away to the projects after school on Friday. Some neighbourhood girls and I gathered outside Tina's second-story, one-bedroom flat she shared with six other family members.

There, on the balcony, I was introduced to Wellastrate hair relaxer. The white cream reeked of harsh chemicals. Tina combed the relaxer through my hair so thoroughly that the teeth scratched my scalp. My skin burned in and around my head and ears. I waited until all the other girls had their hair done. My short hair was sleeked back and white as if I had emptied a bottle of mayonnaise over it. My tobe hung limply down my cheek. But the pain soon subsided under the camaraderie of teenagers primping for a party. Young ladies and men gathered at the community hall in tropical finery. I worried that the after-stench of the relaxer lingered around me.

"Relax, Tobe. The chiadin gel's covered most of the smell," reassured Tina. I wanted to believe her, but she was already signaling Tomasi for a cigarette. Her sincerity was lost on me.

I drank my first bowl of *yaqona* that night. Most of my peers started the practice earlier in life.

"I think Jolame likes you. He keeps paying for you to drink," whispered Tina above the *sigidrigi* songs. Her cough-syrup-red lipstick was already fading from the number of swigs she had taken. Her overdone eyeliner was smudged and I suspected mine was the same.

Jolame wasn't the best-looking guy in the hall. But he wasn't bad looking either. Once in a while, our eyes met across the room. He'd smile and I returned a shy grin. Maybe he would be my first kiss. Perhaps it was the *yaqona* playing illusions on my eyes, but I sensed Jolame was looking at my tobe more than he was me.

My tongue was numbing faster than a dentist's needle to the gum. I sucked on a bonbon to chase the unappetising *yaqona* aftertaste away. I didn't want another drink, but more than that, I wanted to be a good sport. So I drank on.

"Lavenia Kacimarau!" Rarely did I hear my full name outside school or at the Doctor's. Everyone turned to the caller, but I was the first to recognise who it was from voice alone.

My grandparents had returned home when half-way to Namosi, they received a call from the village headman that the meeting was postponed.

Grandma strode into the hall in her purple *sulu-jamba*. At first glance, one would mistake her for another fundraiser attendee despite her age.

Grandma tugged me to my feet. She looked at my hair, parted on the side like a Hollywood star from the golden era. Her lips twitched and her ill-concealed sneer pulled at the corner of her nose. I was so close I noticed the vein on her temple throb. She handled me like a toddler, confident she could easily drag me along behind her, unaware I was already a head taller than her. I'd be free of her with one shove. But the toddler in me was overpowered every time.

At home, Grandma beat me with the first thing she laid her hands on; a metal hanger I left clumsily on the kitchen counter. Hands temporarily tattooed with red channels of raised skin, Grandma ordered me into a chair. Then she did the unthinkable. She brought out scissors and Grandpa's razor. The invisible fetters around my ankles kept me immobile. I hung my head low and watched hair and tears rain onto my floral-printed lap as Grandma razed my hair to the roots. She left my *tobe* untouched. The next day, her mood hadn't changed. If anything, it had mutated into a famished monster, hungry for my humiliation.

Grandpa, none the wiser, drove us; Grandma sat shotgun while I sat on the rexine backseat, feeling like a defeated stray heading to the pound.

"*Kele i ke,*" ordered Grandma, indicating where we should park.

My stomach collywobbled as would a plate of jelly splattering the floor. We were at the projects.

Grandma stood at my open door. "Get out."

I shrank away. "I'm sorry, Grandma. I won't do it again," I pleaded.

"Sorry doesn't erase the embarrassment you caused me last night." When I didn't move, she added, "After all I've done for you when your mother abandoned you…"

I knew there would be no resistance after that. I owed it to her to get out of the car. And when I did, she wrenched away the pompom that covered my naked head. The first tear escaped my eye.

Grandma removed a hibiscus branch from the car boot. With it, she prodded me forward. "Walk."

My knees trembled, eyes downcast as one foot stepped in front of the other. Grandma played the part of a rancher well, driving me like cattle with the threat of the switch. I walked the expanse of the project grounds.

I heard the loud whispers then, the catcalls, the jeers. Young men who acted courteously the night before, now mocked me openly. Jolame was among them. "*Sa qai o Tobe dina qo,*" someone shouted. Part of me was thankful that the cruel laughter that followed drowned out any other callous remark.

Tina emerged from a different flat, still wearing her spaghetti-strap dress. Our eyes met momentarily. She was embarrassed for me, but she stayed at bay.

It was breezy that morning. And as my exposed head felt every bite of wind, my tobe struck my face as if it too had turned on me.

I walked the walk of shame back to the car.

Something withered in me that day. And in its place grew a vapour I spent years trying to form into something that was tangibly me.

Grandpa passed away a week after my twenty-fifth birthday. Heart attack. The *sinu* and hibiscus shrubs grew intrusive and disproportionate. Passionfruit vines tangled among the *jiale* in a territorial fight.

Grandma carried her best memories of Grandpa in the garden. I could still see the ghost of them working side by side; pulling out weeds, trimming wayward shrubs, patting the soil down around a new shoot, and celebrating the first fruit of the soursop tree. It was the child that never left them. It was the grandchild who didn't disappoint them. I felt unworthy and unable to share that sacred space with Grandma.

"A strange couple moved in next door," said Grandma one day.

I knew we had new neighbours but I didn't know the details. Working as a cashier at Shop N Grow Supermarket left little time for me to be more observant.

"*Panikeke!*" Grandma sneered.

If she hadn't been so indignant, I would have laughed. The word was crude and unbecoming in her mouth. If she were trying to keep up appearances in church, she would have used the more formal term, *Vakasaganegane*, to describe the female lovers who had moved in next door.

One word implied so much: *When are you getting married? When will you have children? Are you a panikeke?*

But Grandma and I had never worked up a relationship where she had ease and privilege to ask me those questions. So I withdrew to my room without comment.

When thirty came around, I despised my *tobe*. Virginity wasn't as appealing at thirty as it was at twenty. But I wore my *tobe* with fear and reverence. I felt for it, much the same as I would had Grandma sat on my shoulder like a conscience following me everywhere. One day, I finally said yes to a company party after years of resistance. Part of me still feared that Grandma would turn up and cause a scene even though she dropped hints that my social life should expand beyond work and Sunday morning church service.

We had *lovo*, Fiji Bitter, and Australian wine at the Grand Pacific Hotel.

The Head Stock-clerk, Neori, looked more *uro* by the minute. He filled up the *taki* glass of beer in our circle of revellers, never losing count of who was next in line to drink. Neori's hand lingered longer than necessary over mine as he passed me a *taki*. I chugged the beer, returned him the glass, and smiled with approval.

After a few drinks and *Tuiboto* on the dance floor, we agreed to take our tryst elsewhere.

I wasn't special enough to bed in a plush hotel room, and I knew Neori's paycheck could barely spare a box of Ferrero Roche if he took a stab at romance.

There was a silent agreement between us that a rundown motel room would suffice. He was too drunk to know it, but he was about to deflower an old rose.

It hurt and was not exceptionally pleasurable. But the shackles were broken, and the caged bird flew free.

A month later, I felt the first ambush of morning sickness. Headaches were sickness's standard calling card for me, not a queasy stomach. And though the signs were clear, I dreaded to think my suspicions were true.

I followed Neori outside on one of his cigarette breaks. "I'm pregnant. What should we do?"

Leading up to the encounter, I worked myself up to hope that he would be thrilled and finally cut my *tobe* during our extravagant traditional wedding. And I would wear Grandma's wedding Masi.

Instead, Neori shrugged, killed the cigarette beneath his safety boots, and returned inside. Later, I learned he was courting a nurse from Bua.

I was a single thirty-year-old, living with her grandmother, scarcely making ends meet, a non-virgin wearing a tobe, unprepared for motherhood.

I'd heard rumours of special clinics that could "help me out" at a cost. But I couldn't afford the pills, the injection, or whatever it was that induced premature labour. In my desperation, I went to Tina, who still lived in the projects, now with five kids of her own.

She chased her children outside until we sat alone on her discoloured living room mat, a patchwork of sporadic rips and tears.

"I know a lady in the next building. She's done it to many girls before and they're all fine," said Tina.

"What's her price?" That was the most important question.

"Two number 20 Crest chicken, 10kg Punja's Calrose rice, 10kg FMF flour, 5kg sugar and BH 20."

It was a hefty list, but certainly achievable.

The place of rendezvous was Sobi Park, conveniently situated by a beach where women had been known to rid themselves of an unwanted fetus under cover of a starless Suva City sky.

We entered the derelict public amenity lit only by my companion's phone torchlight.

"Wait," I said. "There's something I have to do first."

I took a tentative step toward the clouded mirror above the broken sink, barely making out my reflection. My hands shook as I raised a pair of scissors to my face. This was it. I stretched the length of my tobe with my left hand. My palm quickly grew moist. In that moment, I felt the years of devotion to my tobe weigh heavy in my uncertain hands. But I told myself not to pity the familiar fuzz of her contours because she had not looked after me as I had her. She had given me empty promises. I had worn her like a crown and she crowned me with scorn.

I closed my eyes.

Snap.

Unaware of the significance of the moment, my companion's voice broke the silence. "This will do," she said as she pushed open a creaky cubicle door. The smell of ammonia and neglect was stronger here.

I sat on the toilet seat as she rummaged in her bag.

She gave me a concoction of bitter leaves and ligneous mystery. "Here, drink this." Swallowing was worse than morning sickness, and I gagged, narrowly managing to keep things down. Within a few minutes, I was drowsy. My mouth was heavy with paralysis, and my world askew with shadows and warped moonbeams.

"Stand up. I need to see."

She steadied me until I found myself standing astride the toilet seat. I could vaguely make out the other cubicles, left and right. I didn't need to see to know they were empty.

"Now squat."

I balanced myself, hands pressed firmly against cubicle walls. Something sharp penetrated and punctured my womb. I cried out.

⌇

When they found me, I had dragged myself as far as the seawall, lying supine, my companion long gone.

My skirt was bloodied. In one hand I held scissors. In the other, my *tobe*.

My pupils remained dilated when torchlight found my face.

In America, Sala dropped a crate of eggs and felt the sudden urge to call Grandma. But she couldn't get through. The Police had gotten through first. They called Grandma as she was putting her wedding masi back into her wooden trunk. Outside, the *Kavika* tree watched on from the garden, still and barren.

Baka Bina

from Papua New Guinea

THE JUDGES:

In a region of many languages [around 1,000] culture becomes the communication tool.

FNWF confronts similar issues when writers want to share their stories in many languages / dialects.

Judges said English is their choice because the stories are intended for the world, not the local village or region. It is their strategy to take the magnificent stories of the Greater Pacific to the world.

For Baka Bina of PNG, FNWF2023 SHORT STORY award recipient, the Judges allowed the three languages. Local language, Tok Pisin, and English. So that Mr Bina's story KAUKAU BLUES could be used at home as well as around the world. A story of bartering for food highlights the counting used in the local language.

The Judges encourage books in multi translations for the local knowledge. They would lean towards helping rather than hindering these stories. For your community, for the wider PNG people and others who Tok Pisin, and then for sharing with the world.

Although Mr Bina is already famous around the world for his stories. And being outspoken about sharing them. We are so glad he shared with us.

KAUKAU BLUES

Baka Bina

D ear FNWF
I would like to submit a short story in trikopi. The same story written in three versions; in **Tok Ples** (a local language); in **Tok Pisin** and in **English**.

This is my experiment of trying to write simultaneously in three languages and I have termed this type of writing to be a 'trikopi'. If it is in two languages only then 'tukopi' can suffice. These two words should be true if all are done by the same author. When another person does the second language by translating it into the second or third language then that becomes translation work and the terms do not apply.

My apologies. For this story, I provide one where each script in each of the languages is between 800 and 879 words.

I could not produce a longer story as I have issues with the Tok Ples. It is difficult trying to write an unwritten language where similar spelt words with stress markers will mean different things and meanings.

Knowing what rules to apply – I have used English grammar rules, but they can be tricky. Secondary to that, having lived away from the village for a considerable time, I admit that I have lost touch with most of the colourful words in Tok Ples plus the doublespeak that underlie these colourful words.

The setting is in a village in the highlands of Papua New Guinea. Traditionally villages would have been a collection of circular hamlets with one huge village communal house (hausmahn) but since the introduction by kiaps (Government Patrol Officers) early during colonisation, a village now tends to be built in a line thus 'hauslain' – houses in a line.

It is in such settings that lives revolve and obviously some infidelity takes place. It could happen anywhere, and these incidents do happen in the villages too. More often now with hauslain. I have tried to create a scenario here as it often does happen.

In this story, I also want to create a scenario where words used in the local counting system are applied and used. For the Tokano Tok Ples speakers, the message is that we do have a counting system that has moved in to kick our own out.

Counting words like nakawosa (stick), asupu (wrap), holokena (wing), ghola (nose), gho (bilum) and mulise (heap or a pile) are not being used anymore in our counting so this is my little bit to use and record it in this small prose.

Could I ask that I be permitted to reproduce this on our face book page 'Let's Learn Tokano', a month after it is, (if at all) published by FNWF. [Absolutely: FNWF]

A. Introduction

B. As I crafted it, 'trikopi' writing a sentence layered over each other.

C. A table showing counting 'trikopi' wise.

D. Tokano Tok Ples version with table of numbers appended.

E. Tok Pisin version with table of numbers appended.

F. English version with table of numbers appended.

This is how I crafted this short story in 'Trikopi':
Tokano Tok Ples,
Tok Pisin and
English.

Baka Barakove Bina
December 2022
A contribution to First Nations Writers Festival

Tokano Tok Ples

Tokano ghamoje liika a ghevena nene ineta ghate'ka ghamoje ine a nei ive. Ami'ne a
nene nike'lone. Ghije iine'ah, a iine tolowa ine a ghateka na'. Ineta napa au ghateka ah
nene uko iine ah nene aveveja hijiki lika na. Pupune ghamoje nene ghate ghate ghijeka

nene ekini ghamoje iineu nei'ike hana oko lika na've. Leli ah nene ne'mi'ne a leli

numutelokati ghamoje-u nene ma ah nene nomive.

Tok Pisin

Ol lain husat save toktok Tokano igat pasin bilong kaunt. Mipela traim lukim. Ol save

usim pinga long han na lek na ol hap bodi bilong ol long bikpela namba. Long kaunt

pasin bilong ol waitlain, igat long tok ples bilong ol na tu em isi tasol long Tok Ples

bilong mip'la igat sampela tasol na ino wankain.

English

The Tokano speaking people had a counting system which started with the counting of the fingers on the hands and toes on the feet and it progressed to bigger numbers using other features of the body. It does have something, but it isn't like the Anglo-Roman counting system which has finite names for each number and it is easier to learn. Our abbreviate ones are not easy compared to the English numbers.

Tokano Tok Ples

Ahmi'ne ghake ghake ghijeka ghamoje nene, ahmene luhuwoh komo mene ghijuwoku

mene heluno ma'mine Tokano ghamoje-u ghate ko nikelone.

Tok Pisin

Dispela pasin blo kaunt, mi traim long putim insait long liklik stori mi mekim long ol lain

Tokano iken luksave long Tokano Tok Ples em tui gat wei blo kaunim namba long Tok Ples.

English

This counting system I would like to relate in a story form so that the Tokano speakers will remember that our Tokano Tok Ples also has a counting system.

Tokano Tok Ples

Ghove Ghotolalo a' Hije Hulo.

Tok Pisin

Toktok Kamap Long Het Bilong Kaukau
Kaukau Blues.

Tokano Tok Ples

'Vena ghoholo, ghove ghano nomonuvone la. Nike na, ghove hamo ma nei he?'

Tok Pisin

'Gutpla meri, mi raun hangere ya. Yu lukim, igat wanpela kaukau oh?'

English

'Good woman, can you see if there is a kaukau? I am hungry.'

Tokano Tok Ples

'Ve maghe, ee'ee Semene melo, yaka ghivise ma u'monenike, gha' no phipilihe, ma lo' na'?
Ghove nene ghosoha seh ta mene nei i we.'

Tok Pisin

'Gutpla mahn, ee papa bilong Semene, yu raun long wonem hap stret na yu hangere. Igat
tupela nupela kaukau istap ya.'

English

My good friend, eei. Why, Semene's father, what have you been doing that caused you to be hungry? There are two raw pieces here.

Tokano Tok Ples

Semene melaho nene monikukoti a'ne nene ghevena yupo numotoh omoi'nite noi.
Muluna ti nene nola nola nomolavoka, ghauno nene mo nene vise lii. Eja'a numuno ah
nene akahe ghijikene nei. Ghaketu kii ah nene milika'aku nene vise iha milima'ne
mineka. Ni'ke ejaga i'ne Melisa vena ko gho nene noi. Melisa vena nene numuno
gha'tenau nene otei noi. Noi toh nene veh ma novi.
Melisa nene nosau ti monikukoti ake noi. Ukonalo intah nene ukona muki toh hite tami.
Ukona mi' ghonoheya ah nene sotoh onoi. Mene veh ma nene ukonalo ghelekake ni'ke
mau ko noi ike ghovemu nene loka noi.

Tok Pisin

Papa bilong Semene raun long em, kamap long hauslain em lukim olsem nogat

mahnmeri. Na tu bel bilong em stat long mekim planti nois na hang're bilong em kamap

ples klia. Haus bilong em lok na em ino painim kii long ples ol save putim long em.

Taim em lukluk go aut em lukim meri Melisa sanap long haus dua bilong em yet. Em

hariap igo long em.

Melisa ikam long ples wara na stap. Em putim klos ino karamapim olgeta skin bilong

em. Papa Semene lukim sedoh bilong meri long klos em werim na em pilim sem liklik

na lukluk igo long narapela hap taim em askim long kaukau.

English

Semene's father had come into an empty village. His stomach started making noises and he knew he was very hungry. His own door was locked, and he could not locate the keys. He looked across from his house to see Melisa put her head out of the door. He had rushed over to her.

Melisa had come from the creek and was wearing a loose flimsy blouse and he could see the contours of her body. He tried to look away from her in embarrassment and continued in the conversation asking for kaukau.

Tokano Tok Ples

'Segha' ne, lamine lani ye. Nike'na, wai nehe? Gho've nene setah ve hamo kisi ma nei i

wokoma, a'minesi nemelipe? Ghano limo nepele hulonoiye.'

Tok Pisin

'Tenk yu tru, em gutpela tok yu bekim tasol inap yu lukim gut, sapos igat planti, inap long

yu givim mi tripela. Mi bagarap tru long hangere.'

English

'Thank you, that is good. Can you see if there are enough kaukau there, you can spare me three. I am very starved.'

Tokano Tok Ples

Mene ve ma nene vena mi gholalo, nene niki ne'ja, ghmoje ma ghotolau tomolave.'

Ghevena numoto nene monema, numuno moki nenen atipe gho nei. Ekaya ine gho

minikesine nei ve. Ghonu ejaga ake, ghonu emega aka, ghevena nene ghonito vii asu

ikene mi ne kane' nei.

Ghijigipe koma koma ma yohi iki mine neja, olitive ghevena li te ghamoje liki minekumu

ghapopo iki ghelema. Olotive ghevena nene ekeja ine gho minikeseine nei.

Mene veh mah nene ghala ghili; vena nene ghamena vai nene vela ghaheva koma tunu

ghonu koma, gholosa gholosa ohe peleka ohe iline ma. Ato numuno okamine ma, aize

koh nene teh onoi ne ma. Ghamoje ghotolau tomolake nene avevejeha ma onaloye lahke

mene veh ma vela lavoha molake nene ghala nene ohte asu ii.

Tok Pisin

Displa mahm ya em lukluk long meri ya wanpela tingting kisim em.

Nogat man long hauslain, olgeta haus dua ipas tasol. Tupela yet tasol mas stap. Em

lukluk igo antap long het bilong hauslain, nogat lain long hauslain. Olgeta lain igo long

ples kot long haraim kot bilong tupela mahn long hauslain.

Ol sampela pikinini pilai pilai istap tasol ol ino givim tingting long tupela bikpela

mahnmeri toktok istap.

Ol bikpela mahnmeri tasol istap. Mahn ya tingting, planti taim, meri ya save givim em

liklik hap ai nogut na planti stil lap long em. Em ken tingim ino longpela taim igo pinis

em ben mekim wankain pasin. Mahn ya ikisim tingting na em stat daunim spet; iau

bilong em sanap strong olgeta.

English

The man looked at the woman and a thought came to his mind.

He looked up to one end of the village and did the same to the other end. The village was deserted. There was a court case up the road between two prominent persons in

the village and everyone had gone there. There were some small children playing butthey took no interest in two adults talking.

The adults were alone. He looked at her and tried to recall the last time she had flirted with him. It was not that long ago. The man felt he could drool.

Tokano Tok Ples

'Apo'ma ke, seloko, ghove seta seta ma ne'melipe?'

Tok Pisin

'Leva, tenk yu, inap yu givim mi fop'la kaukau?'

English

'Dear, thank you, would you be able to give me four.'

Tokano Tok Ples

Mene vena ma ghala ghili. Vegholasa ma nene apo ghulive loka ko, ei'to ghamoje ma neli.

Tok Pisin

Meri ya tingting. Mahn ya kolim leva nem long em ya, mahn mas igat sampela tingting.

English

The woman thought, the man is calling me dear. He must have something.

Tokano Tok Ples

Ukona yopova nene lele okoko ote asu i. Ghala ma ghili. Ghamena vai nene ghonu koma
   koma vela ghaheva tunu ghije joihi emeka noine mah, aahmi a nene ghala ghililihe.

Tok Pisin

Olgeta skin grass bilong em sanap. Tingting Kisim em. Tru em save givim em hap ai
nogut na lap hait long mahn ya. Em gat sampela tingting long despela pasin o.

English

She felt goosebumps all over her. She reminded herself that she does flirt with the man.

Tokano Tok Ples

Mehena emake, ghove nene holoma maloti toko eme lo ye lake tovelapa ine ya, ve nene
ukona lo ote noi.

Tok Pisin

Em givim baksait na laik kisim kaukau long bet na taim em tanim givim baksait mahn
istap pinis long skin bilong em.

English

She turned her back to pick up the kaukau from the bed shelf and when she turned, he was already up behind her.

Tokano Tok Ples

Ukona ma whalala loko ma laka wok woko mene vena ma nene ehelele gholosa vihi ve.

Tok Pisin

Em kisim traip'la poret stret long wonem tevel bilong em ronove igo.

English

She was really surprised and was very fearful for herself.

Tokano Tok Ples

'Vemaghe, ghove voka toh apeloko ma, ghe'mo nene ma ato ineta kumo voka lokonomonepe. Ghohise gholoso nipili inta notaniye ma lo'na.'

Tok Pisin

'Gutpela mahn., mi ting yu raun askim long hangre kaukau tasol yu mekim pasim we mi
swet pundaun ya, yu tok?'

English

'My good man, I was thinking that you were asking for food to qwell your hunger pains but what you are doing is causing me sweats.'

Tokano Tok Ples

'Apo, ghove nene wai oko nemeline loko omo alito nu ye. Ghaka wai ghelemoko, ghove
nene lamine oko neme na.'

Tok Pisin

'Leva, mi laikim yu givim me planti moa kaukau na mi kam klostu long yu. Yu no ken
tingting planti.'

English

'Dear, I just want you to give me a few more kaukaus so that is why I am coming closer to
you. You don't have to worry'.

Tokano Tok Ples

'Ghove nene hamo kumu lape loko ma nene ghe'mo ato ghaka ghele ko nomoneni ve ke
nene vena loka mone lo sa nani ve nanije.'

Tok Pisin

'Mi ting yu laik askim long wanp'la kaukau nogat, yu gat narapela tingting. Yu tru save
raun long askim laik long ol meri.'

English

'I was thinking you were asking for kaukau but no, you have other thoughts. You really go around flirting with women.'

Tokano Tok Ples

'Me'nah, mene asapu to hulolosa nuvo'ne ghove maketi lo tohko volohe loko ma nene ghe
mo tokovoko nah'.'

Tok Pisin

'Em ya, kaukau inap mi salim long wanp'la stik long mama maket, yu karim igo kaikai.'

English

'Here this is some kaukau that I would have sold for ten kina at the market. You can take that with you. '

Tokano Tok Ples

Mene venah ma ghala ghili. Ghonu koma koma peleka nu ohne ma nei'ha, veh'mi numuko nene te'ahma ne nenaje. Toh hoto ikitalijene nene elesha no kohone nenaje. Vena gheleleha noive loko lowa nene hijikeliyeh, iseva loh moloko ghamoje lomeloye.

Tok Pisin

Meri ya tingting. Planti taim mi save givim hap ai nogut long man tasol ol no save mekim kain stil pasin insait long haus bilong narapela mahn. Ol painim ol aut, em pasin weh em ken kisim supsup spia long em. Bai ol mahn pait long pasin bilong pulim meri na nau yet em mas brekbrek na toktok.

English

A thought came to her. There were many occasions she had flirted with him, but today this
was inside another man's house. If they were found out, it was an occasion to be spearedfor the infidelity. A mini war was a possibility and she had to be careful in what she will now say to him.

Tokano Tok Ples

'Seeh, asapu to nene ha minelije, ma ghelena, holokena mene ma nei ne la.'

Tok Pisin

'Seh, wanpela stik larim, olsem wonem, em wanp'la wing moni ya.'

English

'Say, the ten kina, what about this fifty?'

Tokano Tok Ples

'Holokena ka a nene ghevena toghesa toh, toh hoto ilike. Asapu toh ghove mene tokova.
Aato vise lokuvoko, ghevena ghijeva te ikeliyeyeh.'

Tok Pisin

'Desp'la wing blong yu, em bai yu soim long ples bung long ai blong olgeta lain. Kisim
kaukau mi makim prais long wanp'la stik. Mi bai bikmaus nau na ol mahn bai ikam
luksave long mitupela.'

English

'You can keep your fifty that you can show to the public. You take this kaukau for ten kina and get going. I may scream out and then the people will know what we are doing.'

Tokano Tok Ples

'Apo lamine make, ghove voka lonuvone, ghemo ghaka wai wai noghelene, hanuvo'lo'.'

Tok Pisin

'Gutp'la leva, mi askim tasol long kaukau ya, yu yet yu tingting planti long nating.'

'My good dear, I was just asking about kaukau and you are thinking too much.'

Tokano Tok Ples

'Apo apo lamine' loko ghamoje tunu toh hite hite ghamoje lamo joh. Vena loka olosa naine
neiye. Ato ghola nehe, gho ve liki ghonito lo mo mikeka ve nene nomonije. Ato' mulise
hamo kis ve loko to gho la hijiki lo ghijegetali've nanije.'

Tok Pisin

'Yu tok gutpla gutpla leva, na long toktok tasol, yu laik karamapim tok askim laik bilong ol
meri. Yu tru tru laik askim laik bilong mi stret. Mi ken bringim yu igo long kot na inap
long sas mak bilong sais blong nus or ating long wanpela bilum ol bai givim long yu mahn
ya yu stap. Ol inap makim tu sas long wanpla maunten hip mahn yu stap.'

English

'You endear me with your words and cover them with flowery words to hide your desire to molest women. Today you are trying to molest me. I can bring you to court and the charges you will face, and fines will be one, two even a thousand kina to bring to bear on you.'

Tokano Tok Ples

'Apo'. Pipiya ghove kumu no lu je, vena lamine ma ke. Seghane' ghove nene alo neme na.'

Tok Pisin

'Leva, mi askim long pipiya kaukau. Gutpela meri, tenk yu, kaukau, yu ken givim mi o.'

English

'Dear, I am asking for some simple kaukau. My good woman, thank you, can you give me the kaukaus?'

Tokano Tok Ples

'Veh? Toh hite hite ghamoje ve no la pe. Ato mulise hamo tunu ne he' ghoni me'ne hijeka
      toh nai ne ya.'
'Ne mo' nene ghonokahimi venela ma nuwone, ato ve ghonokaho nene ato menelo mi ne
      ote mivoko nolaniye.'

Tok Pisin

'Wonem ya? Yu laik karamapim toktok o. Kain toktok ya bai yu baim kot long klostu
      wanpela bung Maunten.'
'My ya, em mi meri bilong man poromahn bilong yu. Despela mahm poromahn ino kam
      sambai ya, bai yu kisim bilong yu tasol.'

English

'What? You want to hide what you are saying. That type of talking will make you at the
court to pay nearly a thousand kinas.'
'You know that I am the wife of your mate. That mate of mine is not here with me
unfortunately. You could pay dearly for this.'

Tokano Tok Ples

'Apo, vena lamine ma ke, aponehove. Gha' ne' ghelemuvo ghamoje nene toh ko no
hiitenetaniye, hulo nalipe?'

Tok Pisin

'Gutpela meri, nais wan ya, leva bilong mi. Samting mi no tingting long em yu laik traim
karamapim long mi na givim hevi long mi. Inap yu lusim kain toktok?'

English

'Dear, my good and nice friend, you are advancing an idea that I don't have. You are trying to put thoughts into me that will give me trouble. Can you stop that?'

Tokano Tok Ples

'Apo, apo loko ghamoje, toh laneta laneta amojo. Gha'nala nene mololosanai'ne nene
vekalo mulise moloko tohko nomonei'ne nene mene numuto vena alu nene loka oko
togholosa okomikeka ve nomonei'ne nene toh hoto noghotuvo'ne nei'.'

Tok Pisin

'Noken makim swit toktok blo yu wantaim dispela leva toktok. Trouble you laik mekim na
yu bungim long frant blo yu na raun go kam long hauslain. Yu gat tingting long
bagarapim ol meri na pikinini meri nan au mi painaut long yu.'

Tok Pisin

Em givim em hap hait stil smail na pasim ai long em wanpela moa taim na bihainim
desp'la; em opim maus na mekim bikmaus nogut tru.
'Eegghe uugh! Mahn pulim mi insait long haus ya-aa!'

English

She flirted one more time with him and then opened her mouth to scream long and loud.
'Eegghe uugh! There is a man pulling at my hands.'

Tokano Tok Ples

Ghamakilise oko vise luhe lokoma nene alamo vo, vehma nene anatunu velalo hitikake
ana lo gheleha noi. Mene vena mah nene elesah oko veh'mi anau ghelele molo koh
ghakenoi.
Nakawosa nehe asapu nehe holokena nehe ghola nehe, gho nehe alamo'vo, mulise
ghehene kisi nehe, alikeh gho ghateko ghelele lohne.
Mmmmmmmmm.

Tok Pisin

Em i ting olsem, em i bin bikmaus tasol nogat. Mahn ya hariap tru pasim maus bilong
em na meri silip olsem bata insait long hand bilong mahn ya.
Wanpela stik o karamap o hap wing o wanp'la handred o tu, maski tausen kina tu, em
bihain tasol mipela kaunim bihain.
Mmmmmm.

English

She thought she screamed. Instead, the man had covered her mouth and she melted
into his arms. Tens or twenties or fifties or a hundred or two even a thousand kinas, we can discuss
and count them at a later time.
Mmmmmmm.

The counting Chart in trikopi.
Count
numbers in
Engilsh
Kaunim
Namba
long Tok
Tokano ghamoje tunu Ghate
ghate olo'ne.
English equivalent
1 - One Wan hamo One.

2 - Two Tu Seh-ta Two.

3 – Three Tri Seh-ta ve hamo Three.

4 - Four Foa Seh-ta seh-ta ve Four.

5 - Five Faiv Ate helaga One hand – all five fingers.

6 - six Sikis Ate helaga si, ate tolowa

hamo ma loti oluto mo

lavoko

One hand – all five fingers plus one finger from the next hand.

7 – seven Seven Ate helaga si, ate tolowa seh- One hand – all five fingers plus two fingers

ta ma loti oluto mo lavoko from the next hand.

8 – eight Eit Ate helaga si, ate tolowa seh-

ta ve si hamo kisi ma loti

oluto mo lavoko

One hand – all five fingers plus three fingers from the next hand.

9 – nine Nain Ate helaga si, ate tolowa seh-

ta ve seh-ta ma loti oluto mo

lavoko

One hand – all five fingers plus four fingers from the next hand.

10 - ten Ten Ate seh-ta Two hands - all fingers on each hand.

Ghavosa hamo Or alternately one stick.

nakavosa hamo Or alternately one stick.

11 Ileven Ate seh-ta kisi, gizete lakati

tolowa hamo kisi

Two hands – and from the foot, one toe.

15 Fiftin Ate seh-ta ve gizete hamo` All fingers on Two hands and one foot

20 Tenti Gizete ate asu ivoko All fingers on both hands and feet.

Ghovasa seta Or alternately two sticks

Asapu hamo Or one wrap

50 Fifti Holokena - A wing - meaning one part of another

100 Wan handred

Ghola hamo A mountain top/ also nose of a person.

200 Tu handred

Holokena seh-ta Two wings

200 Gho hamo/ ghola seh-ta One bilum or two mountain tops.

300 Tri handred

Gho hamo ve gholasi A bilum and a mountain top.

400 Foa hundred

Gho seta Two bilums

500 Faif handred

Gho seh-ta kisi, ghola hamo 2 bilums and one mountain top - or Two lots of 200 and 1 lot of 100

ghola ate helaga 5 lots of 100

Mulise mi Holokena Literally a Wing to a pile

600 Siks handred

Gho seh-ta ve hamo le

700 Seven handred

Gho seh-ta ve hamo kisi,

amiku ghola hamo kisi

800 Gho seh-ta ve seh-ta ve

900 Gho seh-ta ve seh-ta ve kisi,

ghola hamo kisi

1000 – one thousand

Wan tausen

Mulise hamo One pile

2000 – two thousand

Tu tausen Mulise seh-ta Two piles

*Tokano is deemed a language of its own but is a variation of the Alekano Tok Ples. Tokano is spoken by the ten villages of Iufi- Iufa (Yuhuyuho), Kabiufa and Akameku. A slighter lighter version is spoken by the Ghimiyau/Wande people, and a variant is spoken by the Wantrifu people. These people live from the 10-kilometer mark west of Goroka Town in the Eastern Highlands of Papua New Guinea.

Tokano Tok Ples 'Trikopi' - Ghove Ghotolalo Hije Hulo

Baka Barakove Bina December 2022 for FNWF

Tokano ghamoje lika a ghevena nene ineta ghate ka ghamoje ine nei ive. Ami' nea nene

nikelone. Ghijeiine, ah inetolowa ine a ghateka na-ve. Ineta napa au nene uko iine a

nene aveveja hijiki lika na-ve. Pupune ghamoje nene ghate ghate ghijeka nene ekinito

nei ive. Leli ah nene ne' mi ne a leli numutelokati ghamoje-u nene nomive.

Ahmi'ne ghake ghake ghijeka ghamoje nene, ahmene luhuwoh komo mene ghijuwoku

mene heluno mamine Tokano ghamoje-u nikelone. Ghove Ghotolalo Hije Hulo.

'Vena ghoholo, ghove ghano nomonuvone la. Nike na, ghove hamo ma nei he?'

'Ve maghe, ee'ee Semene melo, yaka ghivise ma u'monenike, gha' no phipilihe, ma lo' na'?

Ghove nene ghosoha seh ta mene nei i we.'

Semene melaho nene monikukoti a'ne nene ghevena yupo numotoh omoi'nite noi.

Muluna ti nene nola nola nomolavoka, ghauno nene mo nene vise lii. Eja'a numuno ah

nene akahe ghijikene nei. Ghaketu kii ah nene milika'aku nene vise iha milima'ne

mineka. Ni'ke ejaga i'ne Melisa vena ko gho nene noi. Melisa vena nene numuno

gha'tenau nene otei noi. Noi toh nene veh ma novi.

Melisa nene nosau ti monikukoti ake noi. Ukonalo intah nene ukona muki toh hite tami.

Ukona mi' ghonoheya ah nene sotoh onoi. Mene veh ma nene ukonalo ghelekake ni'ke

mau ko noi ike ghovemu nene loka noi.

'Segha' ne, lamine lani ye. Nike'na, wai nehe? Gho've nene setah ve hamo kisi ma nei i

wokoma, a'minesi nemelipe? Ghano limo nepele hulonoiye.'

Mene ve ma nene vena mi gholalo, nene niki ne'ja, ghmoje ma ghotolau tomolave.'

Ghevena numoto nene monema, numuno moki nenen atipe gho nei. Ekaya ine gho

minikesine nei ve. Ghonu ejaga ake, ghonu emega aka, ghevena nene ghonito vii asu

ikene mi ne kane' nei.

Ghijigipe koma koma ma yohi iki mine neja, olitive ghevena li te ghamoje liki minekumu

ghapopo iki ghelema. Olotive ghevena nene ekeja ine gho minikeseine nei.

Mene veh mah nene ghala ghili; vena nene ghamena vai nene vela ghaheva koma tunu

ghonu koma, gholosa gholosa ohe peleka ohe iline ma. Ato numuno okamine ma, aize

koh nene teh onoi ne ma. Ghamoje ghotolau tomolake nene avevejeha ma onaloye lahke

mene veh ma vela lavoha molake nene ghala nene ohte asu ii.

'Apo'ma ke, seloko, ghove seta seta ma ne'melipe?'

Mene vena ma ghala ghili. Vegholasa ma nene apo ghulive loka ko, ei'to ghamoje ma

neli.

Ukona yopova nene lele okoko ote asu i. Ghala ma ghili.
Ghamena vai nene ghonu koma
    koma vela ghaheva tunu ghije joihi emeka noine mah,
aahmi a nene ghala ghililihe.

Mehena emake, ghove nene holoma maloti toko eme lo ye
lake tovelapa ine ya, ve nene
    ukona lo ote noi.

Ukona ma whalala loko ma laka wok woko mene vena ma
nene ehelele gholosa vihi ve.

'Vemaghe, ghove voka toh apeloko ma, ghe'mo nene ma
ato ineta kumo voka loko
    nomonepe. Ghohise gholoso nipili inta notaniye ma lo'na.'

'Apo, ghove nene wai oko nemeline loko omo alito nu ye.
Ghaka wai ghelemoko, ghove
    nene lamine oko neme na.'

'Ghove nene hamo kumu lape loko ma nene ghe'mo ato
ghaka ghele ko nomoneni ve ke
    nene vena loka mone lo sa nani ve nanije.'

'Me'nah, mene asapu to hulolosa nuvo'ne ghove maketi lo
tohko volohe loko ma nene ghe
    mo tokovoko nah'.'

Mene venah ma ghala ghili. Ghonu koma koma peleka nu
ohne ma nei'ha, veh'mi numuko
    nene te'ahma ne nenaje. Toh hoto ikitalijene nene elesha
no kohone nenaje. Vena
    gheleleha noive loko lowa nene hijikeliyeh, iseva loh
moloko ghamoje lomeloye.

'Seeh, asapu to nene ha minelije, ma ghelena, holokena
mene ma nei ne la.'

'Holokena ka a nene ghevena toghesa toh, toh hoto ilike.
Asapu toh ghove mene tokova.

Aato vise lokuvoko, ghevena ghijeva te ikeliyeyeh.'

'Apo lamine make, ghove voka lonuvone, ghemo ghaka wai wai noghelene, hanuvo'lo'.'

'Apo apo lamine' loko ghamoje tunu toh hite hite ghamoje lamo joh. Vena loka olosa naine

neiye. Ato ghola nehe, gho ve liki ghonito lo mo mikeka ve nene nomonije. Ato' mulise

hamo kis ve loko to gho la hijiki lo ghijegetali've nanije.'

'Apo'. Pipiya ghove kumu no lu je, vena lamine ma ke. Seghane' ghove nene alo neme na.'

'Veh? Toh hite hite ghamoje ve no la pe. Ato mulise hamo tunu ne he' ghoni me'ne hijeka

toh nai ne ya.'

'Ne mo' nene ghonokahimi venela ma nuwone, ato ve ghonokaho nene ato menelo mi ne

ote mivoko nolaniye.'

'Apo, vena lamine ma ke, aponehove. Gha' ne' ghelemuvo ghamoje nene toh ko no

hiitenetaniye, hulo nalipe?'

'Apo, apo loko ghamoje, toh laneta laneta amojo. Gha'nala nene mololosanai'ne nene

vekalo mulise moloko tohko nomonei'ne nene mene numuto vena alu nene loka oko

togholosa okomikeka ve nomonei'ne nene toh hoto noghotuvo'ne nei'.'

'Nene gho'seleka no lai ne' na. Ghove gholasa ma'mu loka ogetuvonema neine ya, ghe'mo

etami ghamoje lokaneh.'

Ghije koma halekeminine emake, vela ghaheva koma emake, numukuti nene vise nene

hitile koh hulive.

'Eeghe, uugh, ghevena nene numuko mene ghelele ha noine laa-eee.'

Ghamakilise oko vise luhe lokoma nene alamo vo, vehma nene anatunu velalo hitikake

ana lo gheleha noi. Mene vena mah nene elesah oko veh'mi anau ghelele molo koh

ghakenoi.

Nakawoso, yaka na'ne'? Weh, Asaputo nehe holokena nehe ghola nehe, gho nehe

alamo'vo, mulise ghehene kisi nehe, alikeh gho ghateko ghelele lohne.

Mmmmmmmmm.

Tok Pisin 'Trikopi',- Toktok Kamap Long Het Bilong Kaukau

Baka Barakove Bina December 2023 for FNWF

Ol lain husat save toktok Tokano igat pasin bilong kaunt. Mipela traim lukim. Ol save

usim pinga long han na lek na ol hap bodi bilong ol long bikpela namba. Long kaunt

pasin bilong ol waitlain, igat tasol long Tok Ples bilong mip'la igat tasol ino wankain.

Dispela pasin blo kaunt, mi traim long putim insait long liklik stori mi mekim long

mipela luksave long Tokano Tok Ples em tui gat wei blo kaunim namba long Tok Ples.

Toktok Kamap Long Het Bilong Kaukau

'Gutpla meri, mi raun hangere ya. Yu lukim, igat wanpela kaukau oh?'

'Gutpla mahn, ee papa bilong Semene, yu raun long wonem hap stret na yu hangere. Igat

tupela nupela kaukau istap ya.'

Papa bilong Semene raun long em, kamap long hauslain em lukim olsem nogat

mahnmeri. Na tu bel bilong em stat long mekim planti nois na hang're bilong em kamap

ples klia. Haus bilong em lok na em ino painim kii long ples ol save putim long em.

Taim em lukluk go aut em lukim meri Melisa sanap long haus dua bilong em yet. Em

hariap igo long em.

Melisa ikam long ples wara na stap. Em putim klos ino karamapim olgeta skin bilong em. Papa Semene lukim sedoh bilong meri long klos em werim na em pilim sem liklik

na lukluk igo long narapela hap taim em askim long kaukau.

'Tenk yu tru, em gutpela tok yu bekim tasol inap yu lukim gut, sapos igat planti, inap long

yu givim mi tripela. Mi bagarap tru long hangere.'

Displa mahm ya em lukluk long meri ya wanpela tingting kisim em.

Nogat man long hauslain, olgeta haus dua ipas tasol. Tupela yet tasol mas stap. Em

lukluk igo antap long het bilong hauslain, nogat lain long hauslain. Olgeta lain igo long

ples kot long haraim kot bilong tupela mahn long hauslain.

Ol sampela pikinini pilai pilai istap tasol ol ino givim tingting long tupela bikpela

mahnmeri toktok istap.

Ol bikpela mahnmeri tasol istap. Mahn ya tingting, planti taim, meri ya save givim em

liklik hap ai nogut na planti stil lap long em. Em ken tingim ino longpela taim igo pinis

em ben mekim wankain pasin. Mahn ya ikisim tingting na em stat daunim spet; iau

bilong em sanap strong olgeta.

'Leva, tenk yu, inap yu givim mi fop'la kaukau?'

Meri ya tingting. Mahn ya kolim leva nem long em ya, mahn mas igat sampela tingting.

Olgeta skin grass bilong em sanap. Tingting Kisim em. Tru em save givim em hap ai

nogut na lap hait long mahn ya. Em gat sampela tingting long despela pasin o.

Em givim baksait na laik kisim kaukau long bet na taim em tanim givim baksait mahn

istap pinis long skin bilong em.

Em kisim traip'la poret stret long wonem tevel bilong em ronove igo.

'Gutpela mahn., mi ting yu raun askim long hangre kaukau tasol yu mekim pasim we mi

swet pundaun ya, yu tok?'

'Leva, mi laikim yu givim me planti moa kaukau na mi kam klostu long yu. Yu no ken

tingting planti.'

'Mi ting yu laik askim long wanp'la kaukau nogat, yu gat narapela tingting. Yu tru save

raun long askim laik long ol meri.'

'Em ya, kaukau inap mi salim long wanp'la stik long mama maket, yu karim igo kaikai.'

Meri ya tingting. Planti taim mi save givim hap ai nogut long man tasol ol no save mekim

kain stil pasin insait long haus bilong narapela mahn. Ol painim ol aut, em pasin weh em

ken kisim supsup spia long em. Bai ol mahn pait long pasin bilong pulim meri na nau yet

em mas brekbrek na toktok.

'Seh, wanpela stik larim, olsem wonem, em wanp'la wing moni ya.'

'Desp'la wing blong yu, em bai yu soim long ples bung long ai blong olgeta lain. Kisim

kaukau mi makim prais long wanp'la stik. Mi bai bikmaus nau na ol mahn bai ikam

luksave long mitupela.'

'Gutp'la leva, mi askim tasol long kaukau ya, yu yet yu tingting planti long nating.'

'Yu tok gutpla gutpla leva, na long toktok tasol, yu laik karamapim tok askim laik bilong ol

meri. Yu tru tru laik askim laik bilong mi stret. Mi ken bringim yu igo long kot na inap

long sas mak bilong sais blong nus or ating long wanpela bilum ol bai givim long yu mahn

ya yu stap. Ol inap makim tu sas long wanpla maunten hip mahn yu stap.'

'Leva, mi askim long pipiya kaukau. Gutpela meri, tenk yu, kaukau, yu ken givim mi o.'

'Wonem ya? Yu laik karamapim toktok o. Kain toktok ya bai yu baim kot long klostu

wanpela bung Maunten.'

'My ya, em mi meri bilong man poromahn bilong yu. Despela mahm poromahn ino kam

sambai ya, bai yu kisim bilong yu tasol.'

'Gutpela meri, nais wan ya, leva bilong mi. Samting mi no tingting long em yu laik traim karamapim long mi na givim hevi long mi. Inap yu lusim kain toktok?'

'Noken makim swit toktok blo yu wantaim dispela leva toktok. Trouble you laik mekim na yu bungim long frant blo yu na raun go kam long hauslain. Yu gat tingting long bagarapim ol meri na pikinini meri nan au mi painaut long yu.'

'Toktok bilong yu ino kam stret. Yu no tok gut. Mi askim tasol long ol nogut kaukau na yu tok kain kain ya mi les.'

Em givim em hap hait stil smail na pasim ai long em wanpela moa taim na bihainim desp'la; em opim maus na mekim bikmaus nogut tru.

'Eegghe uugh! Mahn pulim mi insait long haus ya-aa!'

Em i ting olsem, em i bin bikmaus tasol nogat. Mahn ya hariap tru pasim maus bilong em na meri ya silip isi olsem bata insait long hand bilong mahn ya.

Em nau, Wanpela Stik o, yu stap we? Ating karamap o hap wing o wanp'la handred o tu, maski tausen kina tu, em bihain tasol mipela kaunim bihain.

Mmmmmm.

English 'Trikopi' – Kaukau Blues

Baka Barakove Bina - December 2022 for FNWF

The Tokano speaking people had a counting system which started with the counting of the fingers on the hands and toes on the feet and it progressed to bigger numbers using other features of the body. It does have something, but it isn't like the Anglo-Roman counting system.

This counting system I would like to relate in a story form so that we remember that our Tokano Language also has a counting system.

Kaukau Blues.

'Good woman, can you see if there is a kaukau? I am hungry.'

My good friend, eei. Why, Semene's father, what have you been doing that caused you to be hungry? There are two raw pieces here.

Semene's father had come into an empty village. His stomach started making noises and he knew he was very hungry. His own door was locked, and he could not locate the keys. He looked across from his house to see Melisa put her head out of the door. He had rushed over to her.

Melisa had come from the creek and was wearing a loose flimsy blouse and he could see the contours of her body. He tried to look away from her in embarrassment and continued in the conversation asking for kaukau.

'Thank you, that is good. Can you see if there are enough kaukau there, you can spare me three. I am very starved.'

The man looked at the woman and a thought came to his mind.

He looked up to one end of the village and did the same to the other end. The village was deserted. There was a court case up the road between two prominent persons in the village and everyone had gone there. There were some small children playing but they took no interest in two adults talking.

The adults were alone. He looked at her and tried to recall the last time she had flirted with him. It was not that long ago. The man felt he could drool.

'Dear, thank you, would you be able to give me four.'

The woman thought, the man is calling me dear. He must have something.

She felt goosebumps all over her. She reminded herself that she does flirt with the man.

She turned her back to pick up the kaukau from the bed shelf and when she turned, he was already up behind her.

She was really surprised and was very fearful for herself.

'My good man, I was thinking that you were asking for food to quell your hunger pains but what you are doing is causing me sweats.'

'Dear, I just want you to give me a few more kaukaus so that is why I am coming closer to you. You don't have to worry'.

'I was thinking you were asking for kaukau but no, you have other thoughts. You really go around flirting with women.'

'Here this is some kaukau that I would have sold for ten kina at the market. You can take that with you. '

A thought came to her. There were many occasions she had flirted with him, but today this was inside another man's house. If they were found out, it was an occasion to be speared for the infidelity. A mini war was a possibility and she had to be careful in what she will now say to him.

'Say, the ten kina, what about this fifty?'

'You can keep your fifty that you can show to the public. You take this kaukau for ten kina and get going. I may scream out and then the people will know what we are doing.'

'My good dear, I was just asking about kaukau and you are thinking too much.'

'You endear me with your words and cover them with flowery words to hide your desire to molest women. Today you are trying to molest me. I can bring you to court and the charges you will face, and fines will be one, two even a thousand kina to bring to bear on you.'

'Dear, I am asking for some simple kaukau. My good woman, thank you, can you give me the kaukaus?'

'What? You want to hide what you are saying. That type of talking will make you at the court to pay nearly a thousand kinas.'

'You know that I am the wife of your mate. That mate of mine is not here with me unfortunately. You could pay dearly for this.'

'Dear, my good and nice friend, you are advancing an idea that I don't have. You are trying to put thoughts into me that will give me trouble. Can you stop that?'

'You don't have to make sweet on your endearments. You are trying to make trouble with all these thinking about molesting the female population in the village. It is never far from your mind and today I get to find out.'

'Your messaging does not come well. I only asked for some pitiful kaukau and you find issues with it.'

She flirted one more time with him and then opened her mouth to scream long and loud. 'Eegghe uugh! There is a man pulling at my hands.'

She thought she had screamed. Instead, the man had covered her mouth and she melted into his arms.

Now, Tenny, where are you? Well, twenty wrappers or fifties or a hundred or two even a thousand kinas, we can discuss and count them at a later time.

Mmmmmmm.

Lorna Saguba

of Papua New Guinea

THE JUDGES:

A poignant and beautiful story. Of young women moving along different life paths, which diverge from those secret whispered plans of their younger friendship. As those plans go awry, we all yearn for those plans of our youth. Or wonder what became of those old friends.

The Judges said "evocative of village life and life everywhere; generational customs; family; and young love".

When she received her Notice of an Award, Mrs Saguba said: "Writers from the Greater Pacific write because our stories like our oceans flood our souls and pour out of us. Most of us are self-taught writers and are challenged by the norms of the mainstream writing and the language skills barriers. FNWF is like the current in the ocean to our writings, our stories, moving them, distributing them to the world. Thank you FNWF". And thank you Mrs Saguba for trusting us with your stories.

This is a magical story, difficult to write so eloquently and we cannot wait to publish it.

HUSBAND / BOYFRIEND HOUSE

Lorna Saguba

It was nearly seven o'clock when we finally arrived at the house. The chilly June wind off the coastline hit us in our faces as we wound down the windows. A fluorescent tube hung at the doorway, casting yellow light onto the verandah where some people sat, and chewed their betelnut while listening to a 1980s tune. In the furthest corner of the verandah, folded up among some rugs, was a bonny little puppy with two sad eyes, like red buttons pasted on his head. The buttons shone for a brief second and then, it all went dim as it slowly lowered his head. Under the house, the flicker from the solar-charged fluorescent cast shadows onto a white sheet hanging on a thin, steel line. And two old men sat on the pandanus mat on the cement, trying their luck with a deck of old cards, betting for a can of coke, while smoke escaped from their nostrils into the chilly winds like chimneys in the movies.

"Is this Jack's house?" I asked agitatedly." Yes." Gima answered, sounding somewhat indecisive.

Gima and I grew up together in a Company's compound; we attended the same primary school, the same high school and now attending the same college together. Our dads used to be workmates. Gima's dad got a new job, so they moved out of the compound five years ago. Gima has two younger brothers and so do I. We were kind of very close, I guess because there were a lot of similarities between us. Some Saturday nights, her mum would bake and we'd go over and watch kid's cartoon and have tea and come back and to our house and sometimes they would come to our house for the same things. Gima now lives with her boyfriend, Jack and his family in the village along the Papuan Coastline; about thirty to forty-five minutes' drive to the city's outskirts.

She moved in with Jack three years ago. I first met Jack when we were in grade nine. He was in one of the boys' schools near our school. I thought he was kind of cute and that they both looked cool together. He was tall and has fairer skin complexion. I think he has some white ancestral connection. There were a lot of mix raced children from the colonial era as the headquarter of the Australian Government was in Port Moresby prior to Independence. There were Polynesian ancestral connections too from the first missionaries contact days. But later, in year eleven, Gima told me that they broke up and she was now dating a Samarai bloke who was working down town. I never met the guy for some reason. She reconnected with Jack again in year twelve and finally moved in with him in year one when we started college.

Now, I called Jack *nakim*i or *naki* for short (in-law) but every time I or any of our close friends called him, *nakimi* (inlaw), Gima becomes really upset and reminds us that he is not her husband but boyfriend. But, Jack, he refers to her as his wife. She thinks, Jack will propose to her and get married to her later.

"If boyfriend, why sleep with him? You are his wife and that is why we will treat him as our in-law." I'd argue with Gima. Trying to drive sense into her. "You are already living with him and the rest of his family. Even Jack's people refer to you as his wife."

"No, no, no! He is just a boyfriend; he has not proposed to me yet." She'd answered forcefully. That was always her reason. The last time, about two months ago when she replied with anger, I decided to leave the matter alone.

But in my mind, Jack is already her husband. I used the term boyfriend just to please my crazy girlfriend but Jack always looked pleased when I give him the brother in-law treatment or refer to him as my in-law. I don't know about the nonsense of waiting for Jack to proposed to her. Sometimes I think Gima is hallucinating, she thinks she is living in Australia or America. Maybe it's a result of watching a lot of movies.

I called my parents and told them not to come and pick me as I will spend the weekend with Gima at her in laws' place and most probably come back on Tuesday to the house. Her parents picked us up at the College and her mother, aunty Karo, gave her two hundred kina and told her to buy some vegetables and our tin fish and meat for the weekend.

Along the way, we stopped at the service station beside the highway and Gima bought a lot of fresh meat, about two kilograms of lamb chops, one kilogram packet of sausage, and few pieces of beef. "I hope there are vegetables at home." I thought to myself. I was tired of eating rice. We had *mekmek* (watery) rice almost every other day at the College and looked forward to eating some fresh vegetables from the garden. I heard from other students that the Cook is *a wantok* (person from the same area/village) of the school principal. This made it difficult to raise a complaint to the school principal. A familiar theory was that we can tell the mood of the Cook from the way the rice turned out in the day. It became almost a humorous thing amongst the students, I guess that eased the pain a bit.

I bought a packet of one-kilogram self-raising flour and a packet of sugar and hoped that we will have some good kaukau, bananas and tapioca to eat over the weekend. She was always asking me to come for weekend ever since we were in year one and it was also about the time she got married or moved in with her boyfriend. This is our final year so I decided to fulfill an outstanding long overdue request.

"Father Dee! Has Jack arrived yet?" Gima called to a man, bare chest and stomach probing out; leaning onto the rails of the verandah. He looked like he needed to support himself on the rails.

"*Lasi!*" (No), He said lazily leaning onto the side of the verandah. "Okay!" Gima called up to him and we went under the house. "That's Jack's uncle', she said. I didn't ask from which side, father's or mother's. We went upstairs and into the mucky atmosphere. The air was thick with *mutrus (tobacco)* smell, and sweat. It smelled like an old cupboard that was not opened for a long time. A wooden bed frame with a single mattress on it was stationed in one corner of the room. The bed's faded blue cotton sheets were pulled halfway out, revealing a gray old mattress. There was a small wooden table next to it, with a yellow, faded photo frame on it. Gima said Jack's grandma sleeps in that bed and the photo frame is of Jack's late mother. I took a quick glance at the photo. She was pretty. Maybe about mid-thirty at the time. She had this big wide, genuine smile on her face. "A bit like Jack's." I thought. A small red hibiscus flower tucked into the long shiny black hair, just near the tip of her left ear, a finishing touch to her long, smooth silky black hair. She looked happy. I see the resemblance now. Jack's white or Polynesian ancestry is definitely from her. The dim light dances on the picture and I shivered and looked away.

"The photo was taken when Jack was about three or four years old at the time." Gima said and sat down on a Cain chair next to it.

I wondered why they did not have other family photos on the walls. Not even of Jack's father. He too had passed away before his mother. Jack is the last of five siblings. He is one of the two boys in the family. I felt sad that a happy person like that is not around anymore. I wondered if Jack misses his mother sometimes. He looks more like his mother. I wonder what his father looked like.

There was a lady sitting quietly on the floor at the entrance of a bedroom. We gave the shopping plastic to her. She wore a long cotton, elastic flowery skirt that covers her ankle and is pulled up to her chest. She could be in her thirties or maybe late twenties. She stood up took the plastic from Gima and smiled shyly at me. Her black teeth like watermelon seeds showing in the dim light. Gima introduced her as Jack's big sister. Her hair unkept and tangling in a mess on her shoulders. There were plastic plates with dried rice grains stuck on them and cups with dried bush shell teabags still in them on the floor. They looked like they were used last night or in the morning. In another corner of the room is a small TV screen on a table he bed, we excused ourselves and went into Gima and Jack's room.

I switched on the light on my mobile phone and placed my small backpack on the side of the double mattress. Yellow sheets still unfolded from the night before. A basket filled to the brim with weeks of dirty clothes on the right side of the bedroom. There is a small window with dusty fly wires. A purple curtain hung over it. There were two big rainbow bags with clothes in them including an old rusty patrol box in another corner. The air was thick. My nose and throat were beginning to itch, my eyes became watery. I have never been in another marriage bedroom apart from my own parents' room.

"I'll make my bed on the floor", I said to Gima, pointing to the plastic mat beside the rainbow bags.

"No, don't be silly. We will use the room for the weekend, Jack can sleep with his family members outside" Gima said and laughed her usual loud laugh.

"Nooo! Not like that! I will not be comfortable sleeping on the floor even if Jack was even in the room. That is total disrespectful in my culture. *Yu save* (You know)." *"Em tambu man ia."*

"Eh! *Wari la*si! he won't even mind"

Jack did not come yet and Gima was beginning to be worried. We went back under the house and I picked up an old torn 'Australian Woman's Magazine' on the cement and looked at the pictures about Western Australia and dreamt of visiting the place one day while Gima called Jack's phone and worked herself into a frenzy.

"Lexy! It's Friday and this Jack should be home already",
She said, channeling her frustrations to a young man of about
twenty years old. He stood leaning on the post, smoking his
mutrus (tobacco) and watching the two old men playing cards.

"He knows that Vavi is spending the weekend. He better
not be late." She added as a matter of fact to herself.

"Erh! Gima! it's Friday and traffic can be a challenge.
Let's worry about him getting home safely not because I am
here." I cut in quickly. *"Yumi stap lo haus ia!."*

"Yes ia..eh!eehei!" The young man laughed at her without
taking his eyes off the men. *"Em kasen blo Jack"* (He is Jack's
cousin).

Come! We go and cook dinner. I suggested to divert her
attention from Jack.

"No! no, you are a guest in this house, please don't worry.
Jacks' big sister is frying our meat." She said, referring to the
lady that we gave the shopping plastic to earlier.

*"Aaai Gima! Plis bikpla tambu meri ia, kam yumi go help, Plis
haus lain bai toktok lo yumi ia."*

"Shh! Don't worry. *Em nogat wok blon em larim em kuk"*,
She whispered to me and laugh.

*"Noken wari, ol no bisi bikpla samtin yu baim suga blon drin
ti"* Gima added smiling into her phone.

"Ia, plis I no gutpla ia, yumi go help" I disagreed.

A small girl came with a big pot. "Can I help you with
something?" I asked.

"No, it's alright, I'll just put some rice in the pot." She said
quietly and went upstairs. Not long she came down with a
one liter of a water plastic bottle in one hand and the pot in
another.

"Plis kam mi helpim yu", I said again.

"It's alright", she said and put the pot on a small table under the house. She poured water into the rice pot and use her sticky fingers from eating an icy pole earlier to rinse the rice and pour out. She poured the second time, into a bowl with grated coconut. Squeeze the fresh coconut cream onto the rice in the pot. She then measured the coconut cream with her middle finger and brought the pot to the fireplace. I felt sorry for her. I wondered if she knew anything about food poisoning. I mumbled a prayer. I hope no one gets sick. She is about nine or ten years old.

"Jakes, what is it!?" Gima shouted at him as soon as he arrived. Jack noticed me sitting under the house and looked embarrassed. He tried to brush the question aside and whispered to Gima. *"Shhh! kar ia mipla waitim ungs mahn lo kam pik ap."* He turned his back to us to remove something from his pockets.

"Wanem hungs mahn, *em go antap long eit nau!*". You should have been here already!" Gima fired back.

"Bruh! You need a chill pill." Jack chuckled, trying to keep the situation down. *"I just told you what happen ia na fon batri too em dai."* But that just made Gima angrier.

I can't understand her, what would be bothering her? I wondered.

"Tambu! Good night!" He called to me ignoring Gima's angry murmurs. *"Unngs mahn go fixim taiya na mipla weitim em na kam late liklik, sori"*

"Eh! Plis, goodnight, don't worry, bikpla samting yu kamap safely lo haus. Yupla stap mi go lukim ol lain kuk pastem."

Gima followed from the back. "This is Friday; I don't know why he had to come late." I did not say anything. The aroma of rice cooked in coconut cream over open fire greeted my nostrils at the doorway of the kitchen hut. For a moment I forgot the *memek (watery)* rice of college.

"Oh wow, rice smells so good on the fire, thank you for cooking." I said to the little girl tending to the fire. "It's getting much cooler in the evening too, isn't it?" I added, sitting down on the *patapata* near the door way. The small girl smiled and pushed a twig into the flame.

"Oh yes, it's always like that, especially at the beginning of May and gets more cold throughout the month of June." Gima replied and retrieved a cigarette from her jean trouser pocket and lit it. She put it in her mouth, closed her eyes and drew in deeply and then slowly releasing the smoke into the night. I was stunned. I didn't know that she smoked.

We sat quietly near the open fire and ate our dinner. Fried sausages and lamb chops with rice. We didn't talk much. I left them and went to bed early. I woke up around 1 am from a loud music coming from the neighbors. Loud noise was also coming from the living room. They were watching a movie, talking and laughing continued into the early hours of the morning. I tossed and turned until 2 am, about the time when everyone else retired for the night too. I slept on the mat on the floor, listening to the willy wag tails.

At first, I thought I was dreaming. But it was Gima shaking my hand and muttering to me to get up. "Get up! Let's go and wake Jack.

"For something?" I asked dazedly.

"I think there is something in the tree." She whispered back with urgency and fright in her voice. I fumbled around for my phone in the dark and pressed the button on the side of it. Light came on and I looked at the screen. It was 3:30am. At that moment, I heard a soft purring coming from the small shady tree outside the window. Gima suddenly collapsed onto the mat next to me. She looked like a frighted small girl. I tried to convince her that it was only a cat in the tree but she was inconvincible. She insisted on waking Jack up.

I don't know what she wanted him to do. Still feeling drowsy, I just stood in the door way with my mobile phone torch switched on. Gima walked stiffly to Jack to wake him. Six people were sleeping on the floor. Jack slept near the main door. She jumped over a few people, as if they were just bag of clothes and walked over to Jack. I was surprised that she didn't go to the side but literally just jumped over the people on the floor.

Jack was very tired and tried to convince her to go back to sleep. But Gima insisted for him to go outside and check. The poor guy got up and went outside, giving me the impression of a small tired, reluctant little boy who is afraid of the dark. I had a feeling that was not the first time and it won't be the last.

I immediately thought of my younger brother and felt really sorry for Jack. Jack is about twenty-two or three, our age group. We are four or five years older than my younger brother. I felt his pain, the burden of being a husband at this age. I didn't think he was ready for that kind of responsibility. I was glad that they did not have children at this time. He came back and mumbled that there was nothing.

We went back to sleep. I don't know if Gima slept. I stayed awake listening to the wind in the trees and the cat that could not go to sleep.

We had pancakes for breakfast. I ate one and drank my hot black bush-shell tea. I saw a small blue tooth speaker in the corner of the living room. I asked Gima if I could turn on the radio and try the speaker. She told me to put the volume up. So, we went under the house to try the speaker of the bluetooth. Everyone was still sleeping including our neighbors.

I turned the radio to FM 100 and the song by Seanr 'Teare' was playing. I put the volume up to medium.

"Pinisim Volume ia!" she said. *"Traim na lukim, em normal ia"* So I did as she said. Part of me wanted to take revenge for the previous night too so I turned the volume up to the end and then quickly lowered the volume. I turned off the radio and went and sat quietly under the mango tree next to the house. I don't know why I suddenly felt guilty about that ten second of loud noise. It didn't feel right.

"Yu bisi lo wanem, em normal ia", Gima laughed at me as she noticed my uncomfortableness.

By mid-morning, all the people and kids left the house. Some went to town and others probably went to other relatives' houses. We were left alone with the dogs. The bony dog kept scratching itself everywhere. Jack went to fetch water from the community tank with a wheelbarrow. A kilometer's walk from the house.

Gima and I wanted to boil rice but there was no one to cut our firewood. I tried but it was too hard to chop. We got some old cartons that were lying around and made a fire and cooked our rice. I ate a little, maybe five spoons of rice and drank some more black tea.

In the evening, we went and pulled up water from a well with a rope tied to a small container to wash. It smelled funny and had some rubbish in it. There were houses nearby and people sitting outside their verandahs can see us bathing. I took my bucket to the back of a pile of banana trees growing nearby and had my shower. Our house was filled with people when we returned. They crowded in front of the television set in the house again.   All talking and laughing at Tom and Jerry's bawdy actions. I pulled out a small stool and sat towards the end of grandma's bed.

Gima said "Don't mind them, they do this every day." I find it interesting that they can laugh at the same things every day. One of the men, probably in his early thirties, a neighbour, walked into the house and immediately crawled into grandma's bed. He pulled up the bedsheets, slept face down and leaned on his elbows, facing the television. His feet towards me. He started laughing along with the rest. I was shocked at his rudeness. Gima made a funny face to me and I stood up and followed her into the room.

"Sorry, man ia kam slip ia em nara neigbour blo Jake ol, kain ol ples type nambaut!" "Oh okay" I said, wondering the behavior of the people. "Is that normal? Or is it just this family?"

We spend another pointless day and I went to bed early. This time, I slept, half-dreaming, half-awake by someone's continuous shriek of laughter or scream in the house until around 2am again and fell into a deep sleep.

Gima woke me up at 3:30am. "There is someone outside, in tree", She whispered urgently and fearfully again. My eyes were heavy, my head throbbing but I went and stood at the doorway again. With my mobile phone torch on and my eyes closed. Making some light with my mobile phone's torch from the bedroom's doorway. I heard Jack's murmurs of reassurances and telling her to go back to sleep.

During breakfast, while drinking my black tea, I looked at my phone and said softly and sadly as I could, "Gima! Guess what? I forgot that I have an important meeting to attend to today, am really sorry that I will need to go today." "We can always do this next time." Gima was sad that I had to leave early and called her parents to come and pick me up. They dropped me off around the lunch time. My parents were out, visiting relatives that day. They were surprised to find me at home in the evening.

My mother asked if everything was okay. I told her I have a meeting and had to come back early.

"Oh well, that's sad, you have a whole semester break to meet and discuss other things. You sounded excited to go and spend time with Gima?" She said as she closed my bedroom door.

I lay on my back on my soft bed. I don't know what is going on in my friend's life. I want to punch her out of this nonsense life. I wondered about the dreams that we spoke about in our primary school days. I recalled her father's words in the car while waiting for Gima to come. She forgot her bilum and went back to get it. "Sister blo yu laik marit so mipla larim em tasol, Yu gutpla yu harim toktok na skul pastem."

She had jokingly said to me when they left me. *"Waitim brideprice, bai yu kam kisim sampla pei!"* Uncle and aunty had laughed along. "Yes! Yes! Bai mi kam!" I had replied laughingly too.

I stared at the ceiling as tears rolled down my face.

Kogora Hale

Of Papua New Guinea

THE JUDGES:

The Judges enthusiastically praised Mr Hale's story as a charming depiction of life in PNG. Small moments matter and we should cherish them, they said.

This short story is magical. Something we all experience but rarely record. Glorious"

The Yellow Butterfly

Kogora Hale

I saw it settle on a grass stalk. A yellow butterfly. For a while it had fluttered in the air, as if wondering which stalk was a good place for resting. Black spots covered the tip of its wings while the rest of its frame danced with sparkling yellow. It floated effortlessly; a weightless creature, a master of the air. It settled now at the tip of the stalk, and proceeded to venture forth with its newfound interest, which was to see if the stalk could arch so far as to reach the ground. I watched with some curiosity, and some wonder, too. Given the queer style in which many butterflies fly, it's safe to assume any attempt to catch it will prove futile. Coming to think of it I hadn't seen any butterfly since I came to the village. What would its name be? I'll call it *Yellow Butterfly* for now, a fitting name.

I took a picture of it on my old phone, just before if flitted away.

~

I had come to the village to spend my last week of holidays at Uncle Tau's place.

Daedae is one of the most remote villages in the Pala district. One thing that sets Daedae apart from its neighbouring villages is its exotic beaches. Four if I have to count them. I had planned before coming to visit all four beaches. I wanted to draw one for my mom, but I had forgotten to bring my sketchbook. Besides, Uncle Tau was quite keen on his new rule of not wandering out except at his word. Daedae had received a lot of complaints about incidents at the beaches and about fights that resulted from young people drinking. Uncle didn't want me to get involved.

So here I was. Sitting in a blue plastic chair. Scolding myself for leaving my sketchbook. Uncle's yard provided a few interesting items I could have sketched. The yard looked spacious, given there were just three of them living here. A stunted sapling stood towards the end of the yard. Beside it lay a flat soccer ball next to a rusting bicycle frame. That would have made a very good sketch. A broken rubbish bin attracted blue flies and a few stray dogs. I had driven all the dogs away except our neighbor's dog. Our friendship would last till dusk when the place was dark and our neighbor's weren't looking. I took a moment to inspect the chair I was sitting on, mainly because of its imbalance. It was already falling apart. Someone had gone to great lengths sewing it together with wire. I was sure the chair wouldn't see the end of this year. The only source of beauty in Uncle Tau's crappy yard was the line of crotons that served as a fence between our place and our neighbor's. That and the yellow butterfly. That was until it had decided to spend its precious time elsewhere.

~

Uncle Tau and Aunt Betty had taken little Richard to the village clinic in the morning. Richard was feeling pain in his tummy. I believe that one of them could have easily taken him to the clinic, perhaps Aunt Betty still nursed a private distrust of the village nurse. Ms. Cathy is an attractive nurse who for whatever strange reasons seemed to like my uncle. I found all of this out yesternight over a late tea session with Uncle Tau. He was a good storyteller who knew how to dramatise his tales and even add more than was true. The latter conclusion I kept private. I wasn't exactly sure which part to believe and didn't think I should ask my aunt.

It was a sunny day, and the weather was scorching hot. I took out my phone and went on Facebook, idly going through the newsfeed. Timothy had uploaded a picture of a German Shepherd. I knew it wasn't his. The local news page of our village "Daedae Press" reported curfew at 10 pm tonight. A couple said they were breaking up, and they wanted the whole world to know. A cheap way to gather needless sympathy, most of them hypocritical. Marry Kelly posted red roses from her garden. Marry was my deskmate during our elementary days in the village. I remember her because she had accused me of stealing her lunch. But the truth was I didn't; unfortunately

I wasn't clever enough to explain to our teacher. Mr. Rod had spanked me, and later dad at home had laughed when I reported the incident. He just shook his head and sent me off. I later overheard dad telling mom I was more like her than him. If it were him, they would have sent him home with some angry teachers because of the chaos he would have caused that day. Whether Uncle Tau or dad was more creative is a matter still open to speculation.

As far as I could gather, Marry owned a garden of roses and many more flowers I wasn't familiar with. Her posts were all about flowers. She wrote a monthly article on her Facebook page about different kinds of flowers. I happen to be a faithful follower. Perhaps had she diverted her writing abilities to something other than flowers, I might have commented on one of her posts.

But I did like what she put out.

There was one about the Hibiscus flower. I only knew, or had always thought growing up, that hibiscuses were only red and that only my grandmother planted them at the back of our house. I was wrong. Hibiscus is a flower native to warm regions throughout the world, and no, it did not only grow in Daedae. And no, there are not only red hibiscuses. There's the pink ones, the white ones, the orange ones, and then there's the ones with colors I can't name. Then there was another about Tiger Lily. I remember thinking Marry had not justified the beauty of this particular flower in her writing. I did not find that post exciting. Instead, I sketched the Lily and sent her a picture of the drawing on Facebook. I had spent a whole week on our kitchen table working on this piece, readily answering everyone that asked. "This one is for a special friend." Mom wanted it on her room, but I told her, "not this one." Unfortunately, Marry Kelly never replied, and my ego was punctured. Punctured so badly it was flat for a month. Marry Kelly was simply a showoff, I had concluded. But I considered her a good Facebook friend as far as her writing regarding flowers was concerned.

Before logging out, I uploaded the picture of the butterfly I had snapped earlier. Below the picture, I inserted the caption, *the yellow butterfly*.

Uncle Tau suddenly appeared behind the house. He wobbled slowly into view, breathing heavily. He had a walking disability that sometimes affected him when he returned from long trips. I was sitting outdoor in the yard, still anxious of the blue chair I occupied.

"Where's aunt?" I asked.

He waved me away, mumbling that they had stopped at a friend's place.

"And Richy?"

"Richy too."

"You didn't want to -."

"Ahhh!" Uncle said, "enough with the questions. Get up."

Uncle took off his sweaty shirt before slumping into the chair. I returned from the kitchen with a cup of drinking water.

"Guess what I found?" Uncle asked proudly. He sipped his water while watching me over the top of the cup. His thin fingers appeared dry with pronounced veins. I was beginning to wonder perhaps the rumors about Uncle Tau's failing lungs were true. But no one spoke about it, as if some unseen law forbids its telling.

"What?"

"A new friend," he said, and then suddenly choked on the water. The cup fell and the remaining water spilled. The butterfly he wanted to show me flew into the air and away into the yard. It was just like the yellow butterfly that I had seen earlier. Meanwhile Uncle continued coughing heavily. Tears welled up in his eyes as he tried to calm himself. He recovered just enough to blow his nose into his handkerchief.

He blew his nose again and then stopped when he heard something like a crack. I heard it too. A sound that seemed familiar. Our eyes locked, and I smiled knowingly. All it took was a moment before the chair burst into pieces beneath him, and he fell over.

We both cracked into a wild laughter. It took a good few seconds before Uncle Tau inquired about the yellow butterfly.

"I saw it fly away," I said as I helped Uncle to his feet.

"It just came and sat on my shoulder like we were both old pals. I was trying to set it free when I found this." He removed a pink watch from his trouser pocket and let it dangle between his fingers.

"I was actually trying to show you the watch." He coughed again before kicking a large piece of the broken chair.

"It must have belonged to a girl," I said.

"Well, it's mine now. Clean this mess up. I'll cook us some rice. I'm very hungry." He disappeared behind the door before I could even take a good look at his watch.

"And Behube?" Uncle called from within the house.

"Yes Uncle."

"While you are at it, can you collect rubbish around the yard?"

"I will."

"Don't go outside," he reminded me.

"I won't."

Clouds appeared in the middle of the sky, just beyond me. I wore a faint smile as I skipped across to the crotons. Surely I would find it somewhere here. Half of the morning was gone. I wished I had not left my sketchbook at town. Then I could have passed the time drawing the yellow butterfly. My phone vibrated.

It was a short message from an unknown number. "Yellow butterfly – The name's Colias Croceus."

I looked behind me. *Had someone been watching me this whole day?* I looked toward the house. It couldn't be Uncle Tau, he was scraping coconut for lunch.   I turned towards our neighbor's house, just in time to see a young girl duck behind the windows. Shelly? Was that her name?

A noise erupted from within and I saw the curtain disappear from where it hung. She must have pulled down the whole thing with her accidently.

"Shelly, what's going on?" A male voice called from under the house.

Idau appeared with a towel around his waist from beneath the window. A shaky voice from inside the house assured him that everything was okay. Just poor judgment on her part.

Idau shook his head and returned from where he came. He had a protruding belly and massive large arms that didn't fit his torso, and he appeared not to care that his towel wasn't tightly secured around him.

I reread the message. Then again. And again. Who could have sent this message? I didn't think it was Shelly. Shelly was just like every other village girl that I came across. They knew how to read but chose to spend their time watching romantic dramas. I remember not seeing her in class after our sixth grade. No, Shelly wouldn't do it.

Several things constituted a quagmire to my ideal plan of enjoying this day. My beloved sketchbook was absent. Uncle Tau would not allow me to go to the garden by myself, or to the village arena, nor to the beaches. But I was leaving the next day and I wanted my last day of holiday to be special. I had no credit to reply to the unknown number. I had some data to spare, though, so I went online and typed "Colias Croceus" on Google. This would be a good time to learn something new. The internet out here in the village is quite slow. I was about to give up when few results began to appear.

I saw the yellow butterfly. Just like the one earlier. *Colias Croceus*. I quickly scanned Idau's house, he was nowhere in sight.

Uncle Tau had the rice pot on the fire and was nursing a pain in his knee. Beyond our humble little dwelling I couldn't see any sign of Richard and his mom yet. Except smoke from Uncle's fire. I took a seat on the grass, happy that clouds had come to my rescue. A soft breeze was blowing and it wasn't long before I was lost amidst different articles.

It turned out I wasn't far from the right name either. *Colias Croceus* was also called Clouded Yellow, a name not far from my *Yellow Butterfly*. Clouded Yellow, known for migrating in mass, and a regular visitor to open fields is one of the very few butterfly species that have no difficulty locating breeding habitats. Clouded Yellow was found everywhere, but mostly in countries like Ireland and Scotland, and Wales. I didn't like the way some of these articles were written. They were so certain this butterfly was an occasional visitor to their place *only*. I imagined inserting Daedae there, just somewhere before Ireland. That way the readers would know half of this passage wasn't entirely inclusive.

Clouded Yellow survive on clover, or trefoil, two common names of the plant genus Trifolium, consisting of about 300 species of flowering plants in the pea family *Fabaceae*. According to these articles Trifolium originated in Europe. *See?* This is what I don't like. They are doing it again. Okay, so how did this Trifolium plant grow in Daedae?

Plus, how did the Yellow Butterfly fly from, Ireland, or England, or wherever those countries are - and arrive here? How can this butterfly fly from one end of the earth, pass the Indian Ocean and reach my country, and for whatever reason track down Daedae, let alone Uncle Tau's house? Especially when it's hardly kept clean.

I decided I was going to post some sort of writing on Facebook later during the night. My personal revolt, titled "Clouded Yellow, found in Daedae, not possible to have come from anywhere else around the world." I imagined several passages already. In fact, I might ask Marry Kelly to help me.

Marry Kelly.

I could picture the satisfaction on her small round face. Her dimples would add to that effect too.

"Excuse me."

I was jolted, and wished that I had not.

"Shelly?"

She was surprised that I remembered her name. Shelly had approached silently and was standing on the other side of the croton.

She had removed a leaf and was eyeing me through a hole in it.

"You were spying on me. Why?"

"Spying? No. I wasn't."

She laughed and threw the leaf at me. I had not yet recovered from the shock, and already she was steering this awkward conversation somewhere I had not anticipated. Idau occasionally glanced our way. I thought I saw dislike in his eyes.

"It's not good to spy on a girl," Shelly said matter-of-factly.

"I wasn't spying on you."

She broke a tiny branch from one of the croton, and began plucking its leaves one by one.

"Idau is not far from us, and he's not a very good person either. I hope you know that. Your Uncle is a good family friend of ours too. If I tell them how you acted this day you might have a very bad afternoon."

My heart raced. I was the little boy in Mr. Rod's class again. And Marry Kelly was here again. Right then I wished I had gone to the garden, or followed Uncle Tau into the house.

Then I saw that Shelly was breaking into a smile. Her attempt to hide it failed, and she succumbed.

"I was just joking, boy." Shelly laughed and pointed with the now leafless branch at our house behind me.

"Richard borrowed our scraper yesterday. Can you fetch it for me? Please."

"Uncle, the neighbors are asking for their scraper."

Uncle Tau was still nursing his knee. He had not fully recovered from the fall.

"I must have broken something when I fell." He motioned towards the coconut scraper. "There, at the corner."

"Uncle," I paused, waiting for him to look up. "Does Shelly have a problem with her head?"

"What do you mean? Something happened to her?"

"She's fine. I'm just wondering if she sometimes acts strange?" He pressed a finger at his knee, probing.

"Strange?"

"Is she," I looked for a word, "like, you know, like sometimes off character?"

"Son, you are confusing me. And wasting my precious time."

I hoisted the scraper, giving up and was about to leave when he motioned with his hand.

"Yeah?"

"She is married, that Shelly. To Idau." He sighed and stretched his arms wide.

"I don't really like the circumstances surrounding her story. But that's life, and we ... we continue."

Idau was Shelly's husband. I didn't find that relationship fond. Nor did I think Uncle was answering my question.

"Uncle what I meant - ."

"Enough Behu. I forgot to tell you that you shouldn't speak to Shelly too, or to Idau."

I left with the scraper while he absentmindedly rumbled on about the rubbish I hadn't picked yet.

Shelly still seemed amused at her own joke when I reached her.

"Was it you that sent a message to my phone just a while ago?" I handed her the scraper. "About the yellow butterfly?"

She shook her head. "I think I must have scared you. I'm sorry."

"It's okay." I said with a friendlier tone. "I also want to ask you a question."

"Is it about your yellow butterfly?"

"No, not the butterfly."

"Is it about my marriage to Idau?"

When she saw I was taken aback she said that all her friends ask her the same question. Some don't, but it's always there on their mind.

"Well, now that you say it, yes." I looked stupid so I asked the first thing that came to mind. "I just wanted to ask if you are happy?"

"I wasn't at first." She looked away at her house. "But I am now."

I offered nothing so she continued. "I love my husband, just in case you think ill of him. Life offered me a bunch of … well, difficulties to say the least. But I have learned to overcome them."

Shelly was offered to Idau when her parents couldn't settle a land dispute with Idau's clan. His previous wife bore him no children and neither could Shelly. They both found out Idau was barren. Idau recently confided with her that he wished to release her back to her parents. "So I'm hoping that I would return soon to my people."

"Why are you so sure he will let you leave?" I asked.

"Because he is a good man. I have come to love him because he has changed." "*Changed?*" I asked, not yet satisfied. "Changed into what?"

"You don't know him. I do." She said defensively. "I have come to learn many things from him. But he knows I long to return. This morning he told me he would take me back to my parents with your Uncle."

"Uncle Tau?"

"Yes. This weekend."

I didn't want to spoil her high hopes. Though I wished that she returned back soon.

"I must leave now. Thanks for the chat." She shook my hands. "When the sun sets this afternoon come look at this spot."

She pointed to a spot on the crotons. "I'll show you something that my husband showed me." Shelly left with the scraper and I quickly went on to collect rubbish around the house. I was glad I didn't take Uncle's rule to not talk to Shelly. She seemed okay.

Uncle Tau was sleeping on the floor of the living room when I came out of the bathroom. I had just finished washing. I stepped over his feet and entered Richard's room to change into new clothes. After serving a plate of rice I carried a small stool outside and set down, hoping some cool breeze will blow in my direction.

My phone vibrated while I was eating. It was the same unknown number.

"Hello?" I spoke between mouthfuls of rice.

"Behube? This is Marry."

Marry Kelly? I quickly gulped the rice. "Marry? How did you get my number?"

"Not important for now. I just wanted to tell you that the name of your Yellow Butterfly is Clouded Yellow."

"Clouded Yellow. Yeah, got it."

"*Colias Croseus* is its scientific name. Apart from flowers I really like butterflies.

And guess what, I have a bookshelf loaded with books on insects too ... Hello?"

"I hear you."

She continued, "By the way, your drawing was nice. I forgot to say thanks because I was busy. I'm a busy person."

"I see," when she didn't say anything I quickly asked, as politely as I could, if I could save her number.

"Yes, you may." She spoke like an unconcerned mother.

"But may I ask again how you got my number?" I was still curious.

"From my aunt. She's the new nurse at the village."

I sat up suddenly. "How did she get my number?"

"Ask your Uncle, and ... also tell him my aunt wants her watch back." "Her watch?"

"Your Uncle would know." She disengaged the call, leaving me guessing, wondering. I concluded as I took my last spoon of rice that Uncle Idau was more creative than dad. That speculation could now be put to rest.

The sun was setting. I wondered what kind of trick Shelly would pull off this time. Then I saw it. A familiar creature. It flitted through the air gracefully. Not one, not two, not even three. I couldn't count all of them. Several Clouded Yellows were filing in. *Colias Croceus*, my new mates. They fluttered in like they owned the place. Up and down they bounced, and then one by one they settled on the spot Shelly had earlier pointed out. All of them. I stood up and tiptoed towards the crotons, but not so close that they would notice me. They all seemed to vie for the same spot, the same croton. The same... the same twig. The twig that Shelly had been holding. My jaw fell ajar. I looked towards Idau's house. Shelly was peeling some garden food and Idau was scraping a coconut. Shelly waved when she saw me. Idau had a knowing smile, and he too waved before saying something to Shelly. They both laughed and Shelly threw a peeling playfully at her husband. Whether it was a private joke aimed at me or to the whole community of Daedae, I cared little. By now the Clouded Yellows covered Shelly's twig. I took my phone out and took a picture of the butterflies. I'd use this as an excuse to chat up Marry Kelly later on.

The next day I returned to town not sure of the many opinions I had always held.

The village folks were not as simple as I thought.

Uncle Idau didn't fare well in his newfound enterprise of lying.

And I think I don't really dislike Marry Kelly at all. On the contrary, she seemed to be nice.

And Idau wasn't as bad as I thought either. But one thing was settled even before I reached town. My next project of sketching would be about my new friend: the yellow butterfly.

Marlene dee Gray Potoura

of Papua New Guinea

There was clapping and yelling when this name for the FNWF2023 Short Story Awards was announced at the celebration in Townsville. As she was the only author present. This was her response to learning of her Award.......

"It is indeed a privilege and I am overly proud with indigenous pride that only The First Nations Writers Festival can understand and grasp - to be part of the FNWF2023.

I tell you, I feel overwhelmed to have sat with Julie Janson, a prestigious indigenous Australian writer, and discussed how I mentor and instruct students at Paradise College, who have stories in The Paradise High School Anthology.

Sharing with my fellow writers from the Greater Pacific, is my greatest love and passion.

As a self-published author and with writing published all around the Pacific and internationally, I see The First Nations Writers Festival as the first and foremost organisation for all First Nation Writers to gather and share their culture through their stories.

Listen up, we in the Greater Pacific have stories to tell. Join us please, I just love FNWF and the writers I have met are exceptionally talented, and are working so hard to keep their indigenous stories alive. I tell you, winning a short story award this year with my piece, 'The singing dogs of New Guinea' is unbelievable. I am still trying to let it all sink in."

Thank you for joining us, Ms dee Gray Potoura. We are so glad you did. A renowned Elder of the Greater Pacific literary community. And an icon for her Nation. An original and classic story.

THE SINGING DOGS
OF NEW GUINEA

Marlene dee Gray Potoura

We moved to Port Moresby and live in House 4 of the 20 Houses on Crestnut Avenue, at the end of the suburb, known as Stage G12, which extends from Stage G1.

Stage G12 is next to the dark tropical forest, which leads to the mysterious Sogeri mountains.

We are from a small - town, and I was used to walking wherever I wanted to go. But here in the city, strict rules are laid out for my sister and me. The number one rule for me is to always get permission from my mother before going into the city.

Port Moresby city can be dangerous if one is at the wrong place and time. Thugs and muggers are looking out for the naïve, and I always let Mum know where I am going.

On Thursdays, I am at the Buffalo Burger with my friends Bryce and Lyndon after our lectures at the University of Papua New Guinea. We go there to eat double burgers and drink a litre of cold Coke each. I love the Thursdays we go there. This was good because I started saving up for those outings and quit wasting my allowances on online gaming.

On Thursdays, my friends and I always start the day without breakfast or lunch because, after 3:15 pm, we usually stuffed ourselves at the Buffalo Burger. The name suits the diner because that's what you get.

For K25.00, you can order a burger with two layers, a one-litre Coke, extra hot chips and a tasty Island salad on the side.

"Max, you seemed to be skipping breakfast on Thursdays. What's going on?" Mum asked, eyeing me over her glasses.

"Mum, they eat double burgers at the Buffalo," my sister answered before I could speak.

Deja is like that. She answers for me.

"Mum isn't asking you. Is your name Max?" I looked at her annoyingly.

"Sorry," she apologised but didn't sound as if she meant it.

"Oh, I think you told me, yes?" Mum touched her chin, trying to remember.

"Yes, Ma, I got permission from you in February to hang out with Bryce and Lyndon at the Buffalo Burger till 5 pm so that Lyndon's Dad or Mum would drop us home after work," I reminded Mum.

"Are you eating there as well?" Mum asked, looking concerned.

One of Mum's essential rules is *not to lie*. She says that once we start lying, it becomes a habit, and we won't feel guilt over it. Deja and I try our best to keep up with that rule, although sometimes, I cover up with white lies. By this, I mean, I may not flush the toilet properly, and then my sister would report me, and then I'd say, 'Oh, the water was off. I think it just came on now.' This was an excellent answer to Mum because Port Moresby is known for frequent water shortages.

And I also think that white lies are okay whenever necessary because they reduce unnecessary stress.

"Yes, Mum. We eat burgers and chill out drinking Coke," I smiled at her.

"That's a great way to spend time with friends," she smiled back at me, then opened her purse, pulled out a K100 and gave it to me.

"Your shout today," she smiled and picked up her bag of books.

"Thanks, Ma," I grinned like a Cheshire cat.

Mum gave Deja a K20.00.

"Your lunch is provided at school. Buy soft drinks for yourself and your circle of singers," Mum smiled and patted her head. My sister and her best friend, Deanne, sing in the school chorale.

Mum is great when she wants to be, but she is a very strict parent. She takes no nonsense from my sister, and I. Keeping our Grades between A and B is a priority. She does not want excuses for Grades falling to B- or C+.

There have always been the three of us, though we only see our Dad during the school holidays.

So, when I heard a *weird tenor* amongst the chorusing dogs at 2 am, I knocked on Mum's door and opened it simultaneously.

Mum is a light sleeper, just like me. She woke up as soon as I walked into her room.

"Max, are you okay," Mum abruptly sat up alert, turning her bedside lamp on. Poor Mum has what she calls a *'two-children panic syndrome'*.

"What? What? Did you hear something?" Mum uttered. "Are you okay? Where is Deja?" She was about to go into panic mode.

"Mum, everything is okay," I assured her as I moved closer to her bed.

"Oh right, okay," Mum gestured with her hands at me to sit beside her.

"Mum, do you hear the dogs outside?" I asked, getting comfortable and leaning back onto the bed.

"Of course, I hear them all the time. They sing to the moon and romance to their hearts' fullest. What happened?" she asked, rubbing her eyes.

"Can you hear them?" I asked, lifting my right hand to indicate if Mum could hear the dogs.

"Yes, I can hear them faintly. This room is way behind the house, so it's vague, Max. Your room is right in front, and the dogs might be noisy. Sleep on this side of the bed, son," Mum patted one side of her queen-size bed and then put two pillows on that side.

"No, Mum, I am okay. Please come to the sitting room and hear the dogs. There is a weird sound you can't hear from here," I told her.

She got up and followed me out of her room when I said that.

Mum always listens to Deja and me. She isn't like most parents who'd say, 'Go to sleep, you are disturbing me' or 'What kind of nonsense are you getting up to at midnight?'

As we walked to the sitting room, the sound of the dogs

was now more precise. The high-pitched shrieking tenor could be heard very clearly.

"What in the world is that sound?" Mum grabbed my left hand as we peered out the window.

"Have you heard it before?" she whispered.

"Yes, Ma, I've heard it a couple of times, but today, I heard the high-pitched tenor broke in between and ended up into a coughing fit," I whispered back at Mum.

Mum stared at me in puzzlement.

"What? Is that so? Now, that's quite weird," she turned again and looked out the window.

"That dog might be ill; therefore, it is not vocalising their chorus but sobbing it. That coughing fit is strange." Mum stated as she quickly pulled the curtains tightly together.

"The coughing is truly strange," I agreed as I followed her into the kitchen to get a glass of water. What she explained made sense.

"Maybe, it's a female dog, who got dumped by the alpha," Mum laughed and gave me a glass of water.

"Thanks, Mum. Maybe so," I chuckled, trying to join Mum's lampoon humour.

"But Mum, there is a similarity between these dogs and the dogs from our Island home," I informed her.

"Oh, those mountain dogs you talked about when you returned from your holiday? They've been there for ages. Goodness knows for how long," Mum threw her hands in the air expressing that the wild dogs in the mountains and valleys have been there since the earliest.

I have been hearing dogs vocalising since I was a child. In the small town where I grew up, we would chase them off the streets and fields to get rid of their gatherings, which most folks found annoying. An older relative once came from the village to visit us, and I asked him if there were dogs like that in our villages on Bougainville Island, and he said, "Yes. In our villages, the dogs have been vocalising like that since the beginning. These dogs are another race who must keep up with their rituals." I have always remembered his explanation, and Mum added that he was a man who loved animals and respected their behaviours.

Two years after our relative told me about the dogs, I convinced Mum to send me to Bougainville Island to spend my Christmas holiday in our village. That was three years ago, before moving to Port Moresby.

The ones I had heard were wild dogs. They sounded like banjos strumming in the mountains, and the sound echoed everywhere, bouncing off rocks and creating mystical tunes in the villages below. It was an experience of a lifetime that taught me to respect dogs at a high level, as there are reasons why they are known as men's best friends.

While in the village, I asked Uncle Caleb about the banjo-like sounds from the mountains. He told me that wild dogs have their gathering places and go there for a purpose. He also stated that when wild dogs' choruses are heard in the forests, it is considered sacred, and people from the villages pay special attention respectfully. This attention is that people have ignored these animals for generations, respecting their privacy and not bothering them. There is an unspoken silence of a respectful oath to leave them in peace. Because there is something out there, they say, and as humans, we should all be fine with, or else the balance in the elements would tamper.

Mum and Uncle Caleb told me what people in our village say to their children. This kind of talk has been passed down for generations.

"They do not cause any harm, so throughout time, humans have left these wild dogs alone and not entered their gathering places," Uncle Caleb had clarified.

"The wild dogs gather only at night. They are nocturnal creatures," Uncle Caleb continued to emphasise seriously.

"Max, you will see that when the wild dogs start their choruses, domesticated dogs suddenly prick up their ears, listen for a second or two, and then whimper. After whining for a few minutes, they curl themselves into crescents and go to sleep," Uncle Caleb indicated, pointing to Mala, the dog that loafed around the village.

"Why do domesticated dogs do that?" I had asked curiously.

"They are afraid," Uncle Caleb whispered. "Humans and their dogs are afraid of the wild dogs." The information I gathered from Uncle Caleb had me conclude that humans' respect for wild mountain dogs is immense.

After talking to my uncle, I noticed the dogs' howling' in Lae town. I started to sense the uniqueness and the sacredness that came with it. The howling was not ordinary to me anymore. I could tell the difference between the howling and the chorusing.

When the chorusing was happening, there was no howling. Uncle Caleb was right.

But with these dogs in Port Moresby city, I knew something weird was happening. It was bizarre that the high vocalising tenor broke into a coughing fit, which didn't even stop the other dogs from chorusing until they finished humming monotones.

I heard the dogs throughout the weeks but didn't hear the high-pitched tenor. I kept wondering why the dog with the weird vocals was not in the group anymore. Maybe Mum was right. Maybe the dog was ill and was sobbing about the sounds. Perhaps the poor dog died somewhere? This thought kept gnawing at me, so I told my friends on Thursday during our outing at Buffalo Burger.

"Hey, you are new in this city, Max. Weird encounters are always popping down from the mountains into Stage G-12," Lyndon informed in a low voice.

"But you don't live in G-12, Lyndon. How do you know?" I asked to get more out of him. Lyndon's Dad is a Lieutenant in the army, so he lives at the army barracks.

"My Dad and his platoon fished out a huge black python stuck in the main drain at G-12. The python had swallowed a dog and then got stuck as it tried to slither through the drain back to the dark forest," Lyndon indicated with his fork pointing to the mountains, evident in the horizon from where we were sitting.

"When did this happen?" I alarmingly looked at Lyndon and then at Bryce.

"It happened last year. Other strange stories connect G-12 to the dark forest and the Sogeri mountains," Lyndon continued looking back at Bryce and me.

"Tell us the weirdest one, Lyndon," Bryce told him as I nodded in agreement.

Bryce lived on Lilac Avenue at G-12. He was new to the city too, as his Mum is a lecturer and had moved to the city two years ago. I lived on Crestnut Avenue, on Magana Street. We were both stuck in G-12. I didn't mind the stories. I just wanted to hear them to make sense of what was bothering me.

"Some years ago, a Caucasian woman emerged from the dark forest; most believed she walked down from the mountains in strange clothes. She wore a long dress and had a bonnet on her head. She had on high boots and a weird umbrella. She was spotted on Magpie Avenue looking lost and confused. The people who lived there asked her if she was all right. She spoke English, but her dialect and accent were strange and difficult to understand. She was reportedly dazed, scared and confused, murmuring, 'Toupin'. As noon approached, she was finally taken to the Police Station. She was detained there, and when they gave her rice and beef stew with salad, she looked at the food in disgust, again saying the word 'Toupin'. During the night, a cup of coffee was offered to her. She tasted it and spat it all out. She sat on a chair and muttered words and explanations that did not connect to any continent. She gestured to use the Ladies' Room, and when she was shown the lavatory, she stared at it in confusion. They left her there to do her business which she did for a long time. A female police officer was told to check on the woman, but when the police officer entered the female restroom, the Caucasian was not there. They looked everywhere and needed help to figure out how she would have left the ablution block or gone past many police officers without being noticed. No one ever saw her again." Lyndon finished off and sipped his Coke through a straw.

"That is the strangest, creepiest tale I've ever heard, Lyndon," Bryce muttered.

"Strange indeed," I added, looking around the diner.

There is Magpie Avenue, Lilac Avenue and then Crestnut Avenue. These streets were next to the forest, lined alongside, facing the mountains.

"And who told you this story, Lyndon?" I asked him.

"My Mum," he answered, slurping his drink through a straw.

"Who told the story to your Mum?" Bryce asked.

"My Mum was the female police officer."

Bryce and I looked at each other in shock.

That evening, I asked Mum why she chose to live in Stage G-12 instead of other parts of the big city.

"Housing in G-12 is affordable son. I cannot afford the high rentals in other parts of the city. We will continue to live here until a house is available at the school campus," she explained in two sentences that made good sense to me.

In July, the tropical rains started, and it rained straight for two weeks. The drains flooded with debris that overflowed onto the roads. Mum told Deja and me to stay home until the city authorities cleared and cleaned the streets. We stayed home for two days. I lounged on the couch, dozing off at times and watching anacondas in the US Glades on NATGEO WILD while Deja practised her songs in her room.

When the rain stopped, the stars were evident in the night sky. Mum and I sat on two deck chairs out on the lawn, sipping ground coffee and talking about school and hoping it wouldn't rain for a month.

It must have been the coffee plus the amount of sleep I had during the two days because I couldn't sleep that night. I got on Google, read about the US glades, and decided that I preferred my country with a tropical climate and rain forests.

At around 1:30 am, I went to the bathroom, and as soon as I came out and closed the door, *the high shrieking tenor was once again outstandingly vocalising* right outside on the street next to our house. I stopped in my tracks and listened.

This time, the dogs' vocalisation was weirdly harmonised and sounded *organised*. I decided to go out and check.

The dogs were right outside the fence on Magana Street. Their vocalising was ear-piercing and weirdly soothing. The high-pitched tenor was at its best. It held the key on a high note and kept it going there. Then it flattered and broke out in coughing fits. I quickly looked around, put my eye onto the hole in the fence, and looked out.

About six dogs were moving around in the shadows. I reached out to move the bolt, and my hand hit the standing seam. The noise in the silence of the night was quite loud. I saw weirdly shaped dogs scampering into the shadows. Now that truly piqued my curiosity.

In the morning, my friends came over at around 7:30 am. As we sat around the table chatting after breakfast, Mum handed her students' assignments to us.

"Read through these analytical reviews on the biographical film Black Harvest by Bob Connelly and Robin Anderson and write your comments on the sticky notes and paste them at the bottom of the papers," she instructed.

Black Harvest was a film about Joe Leahy, a half-caste son of one of the first explorers of the Papua New Guinea interior. He was a coffee grower in the Nebilyer Valley from the land he bought from the Ganiga people.

"I still believe Joe Leahy conned the Ganiga people," Lyndon stated as he flicked through the reviews.

"He never conned them. They all agreed to work as partners, but there were two main downfalls. One, the coffee prices dropped, and two, the Ganiga men were involved in the tribal fights, helping a mutual tribe and did not pick the coffee fruits. Therefore, the coffee fruits blackened and rotted on the trees," Bryce said.

"Tribal fights are always causing downfalls in the highlands of New Guinea," I added.

"A scientist captured some singing dogs around that region for research or something," Bryce informed us.

Lyndon and I looked at him in bafflement.

"I looked it up on Google because you've been hearing weird dogs vocalising in chorus," he shrugged.

Lyndon and I sat there looking at Bryce.

"Wow," we both said in unison.

Bryce is an all-A+ student because of the way he is. He loves doing research, exploring and finding answers. He is intuitive and extraordinary. Mum usually gives him her students' reviews and summaries. He reads and writes comments on the sticky notes she leaves at the bottom of the papers.

A few months back, Mum asked him to view an ethnographic film from Pakistan and write an analytical review. He did an exceptional write-up, which Mum talked about for days. Mum loves Bryce's mind as she says, 'He is a genius or just a ravenous study body.'

"He is brilliant, must be from his Mum, I think. She is a lecturer at the university." Mum praises Bryce all the time when he comes to our place.

"My Mum is an anthropologist. She lectures in anthropology," he told Mum once when she asked what his Mum's profession was.

For the whole week, the dogs continuously vocalised outside my room in an organised and unnatural manner.

"Ma, the dogs in this city are annoying," I informed Mother over breakfast. "I am tired of hearing their weird howling every night."

"These dogs can change pitch when they howl. They are vocalising Ma. They are different from the ones I have heard in Lae town. They are like the wild dogs from the valleys in our village," I continued chatting, referring to the small town we previously lived in before moving to the city.

"Oh yes, they are different," Mum agreed, clapping her hands to show that something had just clicked in her mind. "When you woke me that night about the weird coughing sound the dog was making, I decided to find out. They must be the endangered species known as the New Guinea singing dogs. There is a whole lot of research about these dogs on Wikipedia. I believe they come down from the Sogeri mountains to sing to us" Mum smiled at me as she flipped through her Language and Literature exam papers.

"Ma, what else did you read about the singing dogs?" I scowled questioningly.

"The New Guinea singing dogs are the rarest dogs in the world. They move like cats and can climb trees. They can also squeeze through small openings, as their spines and muscles are put together differently than most dogs. Their flexibility also allows them to toss their heads 360 degrees. They are predators and very independent," Mum explained, sipping her coffee.

"The article said that these are healthy dogs with soft coloured coats that range from red to brown, and they have a life span of 15 to 20 years."

Night after night, the high-pitched tenor and the monotones overwhelmed me to my wit's end. These dogs were singing their odd tunes right next to my room as if to prove what I already knew was true. And when they sang together, it sounded like a rehearsed chorus.

I felt it was like a call; a message was being sent to me.

I just discovered that a rare breed of dogs known as the New Guinea singing dogs was written about on Wikipedia as I was instead focused on traditional beliefs shared by Uncle Caleb.

But Mum and Bryce had proven that the New Guinea singing dog exists.

The chorus was already in my head, and I even hummed the tune while taking notes through my lectures at the University of Papua New Guinea.

I told my friend Bryce who lived on the next street that the dogs were disturbing me.

"Have you heard them?" I asked him.

"Not really. I hear barks and a howl now and then," he answered.

"There is a dog with a high-pitched tone. Have you heard it?" I asked him again

"Naaah, I have not heard any dogs howling late at night. It's funny, though, because I often stay up late," he stated, touching his chin.

That is the thing in New Guinea. People hear them so often that it becomes part of them, and they take no notice whether the dogs are vocalising a detectable chorus or are howling nonsense to the moon.

~

That night, the full moon was high and shone brightly as feather-like clouds pivoted across the night sky. I listened to the dogs' singing outside on Magana Street. The high-pitched tenor broke into a coughing fit, which didn't stop the other dogs' vocalising until they continued and finished into humming monotones.

I grabbed my capote from the wardrobe, picked up my phone, put it in my jeans pocket, maneuvered behind the cabinet, pulled out my baseball bat and crept out the front door. I pushed my feet into my sneakers, crept down the stairs furtively, and tiptoed as softly as possible to the corrugated fence peephole.

The dogs were on the street right outside the fence. Their choruses were ear-piercing and peculiar. The night sky was mesmerising, making me feel like it connected me to an extraordinary journey. I was suddenly reminded of the musical tune at the beginning of the sci-fi series The X-Files. I felt the dogs were hinting that something out of the ordinary was about to emerge. I felt light-headed and magnetised.

And on that night, the high-pitched tenor was at its best. It held the key on a high note and kept it going. Then it fluttered and broke out in coughing fits. I quickly looked around, put my right eye onto the hole in the fence, and looked out like I had done earlier, careful this time not to touch the bolt.

I counted around eight strange-looking dogs outside, next to our fence. Strange in a way that they were slim and had large heads. Then I saw the weirdest one. It was smaller and longer in the middle, with a much larger head. It stood there and stared at the moon – in an intelligent manner. They were waiting. It was obvious to me.

I took my eye out of the peephole in shock and disbelief for a second, wondering if I saw what I saw. The chorus started again, so I put my eye back on the peephole and looked out.

The dogs had their faces pointed upwards in chorus. I fixed my eye on the peephole and focused on the dogs. The oddest one looked down while the others vocalised together. I watched as the singing dogs came into a monotone, and then the unusual one lifted its head, opened its mouth, and the high-pitched tenor came out of it. It held the tune there and kept it going, and as his other friends came into humming banjo-like sounds, the dog cut the pitch and dropped it. Damn! I couldn't believe it. These dogs were organised.

The security light from our yard illuminated the street, and I could see the dogs visibly. I saw the oddest-looking dog move among the others, make growling noises. Then as if on cue, it jumped into the light, and I was taken aback, ghastly horrified, bumping the corrugated fence. The dogs sped off, scampering down the dark street. I got up from where I was and stood momentarily, trying to organise my thoughts.

Did I see what I just saw?

I decided to go out of the gate and try to see where the dogs were headed. I had to find out what was going on.

I walked down Magana Street, onto Crestnut Avenue and then to Lilac Avenue. I was curious about the street the dogs had taken, but I just walked. I also wasn't sure what I was looking for; I just decided to see where the dogs had gone and tried to get a good look at the oddest one. I realised that the dogs had manes like lions do. Deep in my mind, I realised the dogs were organised and up to something. I also wanted to catch them doing something out of the ordinary.

I was right. Today, I know, I was chosen and got pulled into it.

As I walked past Bryce's house, I saw him up on the roof of his cubby house, looking at the night sky through his telescope.

The thing about Bryce is that he is not an early sleeper. He is studying Quantum Physics at the university. He is also insanely obsessed with astronomy, so he has this telescope he observes the night sky. Once, he told me he was trying to communicate with other beings from other universes.

"How can you communicate with these beings if you can only spot them discernibly through the telescope?" I asked him.

"My theory is that all beings in the universe are way more advanced than us. They have technology that takes them through space in minutes. It is quite obvious to them that I am trying to get to them through space study, but I will only make contact when I find the cryptic code that holds the molecules somewhere in the alignment of the night clouds. I am still learning, and one day I will crack it."

Bryce boggles me with his readily made theories of living beings on Earth and beyond the universe. He always seems to have a theory for a defect or rarity of nature in New Guinea.

I stood in the dark, behind the gate and dialled his number. I saw him in the clear tropical night as he put his hand into his left trouser pocket to pull out his phone.

"Hey Bryce, you will not believe what I just saw a few minutes ago," I couldn't contain the shock mixed with the excitement of adventure.

"What happened? What did you see, Max?" Bryce half yelled into the phone.

"Bryce, I saw the high-pitched tenor tonight," I could feel my hands shaking with the phone, and my knees were hurting for no reason. I also realised that I was carrying my prized baseball bat, the one I had named *Homebase 3000*.

"Oh, the high tenor you told me about? What kind of dog is it?" he yelled into my phone.

"It's a grotesquely distorted mutt with an extra-long body and a lion-like mane," my voice shook with the excitement of discovery.

"NOOOO! Come on, bro, what kind of nonsense is that?" Bryce yelled into my ear.

"Calm down. I am at your gate right now. Come as silently as you can," I whispered into the phone.

Bryce casually walked over to the gate and came through the smaller one. We stood huddled under the Earleaf Acacia.

"Good grief, Max. You are out of your house after 2 am?" I knew that was a rhetorical question because, as he could see, I was with him, standing in the shadows outside his house.

I recounted to him what I had seen earlier.

"That, my friend, is not a dog," Bryce stated in a low, matter-of-fact voice. I looked at him alarmingly. He somehow sensed my look of confusion in the darkness.

"Those are not real dogs. They are aliens coming through a portal, and as they enter our world, they are transformed into dogs. But because of the force of gravity, they are stretched, and their heads are deflated," he explained pretty confidently.

"How the hell do you know that?" I was overwhelmed with confusion. "These dogs are the New Guinea singing dogs," I whispered fiercely. But in my mind, I knew they did not resemble my Mum's description.

"It is my theory, Max," he retorted, pulling me closer to the tree trunk as the scampering of feet became visible to our ears.

We looked down Lilac Avenue.

"What the heck!" I muttered as I moved behind the tree trunk, and at the same time, Bryce pulled me down.

We watched the dogs charging at full speed up the street. They were chasing something. Or were they being chased by something?

They went past where we were hiding and stopped around twenty metres from us. As we watched, all the dogs got behind a taller dog that stood up, stretched out and bent down its mane.

"Oh my gosh, Bryce, that's the high-pitched tenor dog," I whispered as we watched silently.

"Oh wow, it has presence," Bryce whispered back.

Bryce was correct. That dog was in authority and knew what it was doing.

The dogs started chorusing in lyric baritones that sounded like bass banjos. The sound was advanced but similar to what I heard in my mother's village. Then the dog with the mane pointed its face upwards, opened its mouth, and the high-pitched tenor came out – in a high shrieking note. And with the banjo bass from the other dogs, the sound was truly mesmerising. It rang through our ears, vibrating our heads and shaking our bodies.

Bryce and I watched silently in awe, which was mixed with blatant fear.

Amidst the dogs' vocalising, another sound entered our ears—a deep rumbling sound from Crestnut Avenue.

"Oh, cripes," Bryce mumbled as he grabbed my left hand. I held on to my baseball bat in my right hand and held his right hand with my left hand as we looked down Lilac Avenue. The tropical night was evident as the moon and clouds raced across the sky, obviously bothered by what we witnessed.

A thick black smoke emerged from Magana Street, rolling onto Crestnut Avenue. It spilled over to Lilac Avenue and rolled down the main street, making eerie rumbling sounds.

The thick black smoke stopped around twenty metres away from where we were. It started moving but was pulled back by something we couldn't see. We watched as the black smoke struggled to move forward while the deep, rumbling, eerie sound rolled grinding noises.

We were glued to the ground next to the trunk of the Acacia, frozen in fear.

Then I realised what was happening.

"Bryce, the dogs are pushing the black smoke back with their chorus," I whispered.

The dogs supported the high-pitched tenor with their deep baritones. The high-pitched tenor kept it going at the highest pitch, which sounded more like a screech. I kept saying, 'Please don't break into a cough, please don't break into a cough', because now I understood what the dogs' chorus was intended for.

The black smoke oozed out an aura of pure evil.

The thick blackness was stuck there, though it wanted to move forward.

The high-pitched tenor did not break into a cough but dropped the pitch as the baritones changed to low monotones. The black smoke started rolling forward again, and was just a few steps away from us when the high-pitched tenor picked up again with the highest pitch while the other dogs changed into deep baritones.

The sound was deafening as the dogs forced the black smoke rooted right next to where we hid behind the Acacia.

The black smoke started spilling sideways. We were

terrified as we held on to each other and crouched as low as we could.

I looked closely and saw something silvery cascading like the liquid mercury, with two sparkling slanted red dots twirling restlessly inside the smoke. It was the most sinister, frightening sight I had ever seen. I knew the fiery eyes were on us.

"There's a serpent twirling in the smoke, trying to get out," I heard Bryce whisper.

The dogs' chorus sounded like an orchestra dominated by banjos and a conspicuous violin that played at the highest note. We put our pointers into our ears and crouched as low as possible, watching intently as the two fiery eyes rolled in the thick mass, forcing them to come straight for us.

Right before our eyes, the black smoke exploded into a blinding light, shredding it into fragments of unrecognisable substances. The high-pitched vocalist stopped straight out, and the monotones continued humming into silence.

On Tuesday at around midday, I woke up on a crisp white bed at the Port Moresby private hospital.

Mum was there, and she told me that a man named Tau found Bryce and me under the Acacia tree in deep slumber between 6 – 7 am yesterday on Monday morning. He thought we were dead because Bryce had blood on his face and blisters on his arms. He looked closely at me and saw blisters on my face, but my arms were safe because I had my capote on. He then realised we were still breathing, so he banged Bryce's gate, waking his mother. An ambulance was called, and we were taken to the hospital.

Mum told me we were put in separate private rooms because the doctors wanted to get the story out of us individually and not as companions. When I gathered the story from my Mum, I put two and two together and concluded that they agreed with the police as they might have suspected us of arson.

The hospital staff were confused about the strange blisters. From how Mum was raving on, I realised she thought we were involved in some first-year university initiation that went wrong.

When Mum left, the doctor asked me what had happened. I didn't know how to answer.

"Did you gather dry grasses in the middle of the street and start a fire?" he asked softly.

I didn't answer.

"Well, Max, Bryce said, you saw what happened," the doctor continued.

At that moment, I realised that Bryce wanted me to answer the questions. It was a sign that he wanted me to give them a story.

I told Doctor Banna. "Someone had already lit the dry grasses in the middle of the street next to Bryce's house. I was with Bryce, studying the night sky through his telescope, and we saw the fire and tried to put it out. Still, an unknown substance in the fire exploded, and I think it caused us to fall unconscious on the side of the Earleaf Acacia," I tried my best to explain without sounding vague. White lies are okay when people wouldn't understand the situation.

No one would believe what we encountered on Sunday night.

"All right, that makes sense. Your burns are not severe, but they are odd. I still cannot determine what chemical caused you the blisters," Doctor Banna observed, touching my face puzzledly.

We had seen what we were not supposed to see. No one would ever believe that we had encountered dogs who sang in an organised chorus and had exploded an evil roll of black smoke – a cocoon to an evil being - to smithereens.

Those bloody dogs were unique. I hold nothing but respect for the high-pitched tenor and the banjo baritones.

Or did I cross into another dimension, dragging my friend into it? I am still mystified.

A phone started ringing. I looked at the table beside the bed and saw my phone there. I reached out and picked it up, looking at the caller.

It was Mum.

"Hey, how are you doing?" she asked cheerfully. I could hear her chopping something. She had gone home to cook lunch for my sister and her friends.

"I am okay, Ma. I just remembered something. Can you please send Deja and her friends to Lilac Avenue to search for my Homebase 3000? It should be under the Acacia tree next to Bryce's house."

"Oh, we were just admiring your *Homebase 3000*, Max. You left it at home on the bench downstairs. The lettering *Homebase 3000* is clear around the base. When I got home, Deja and her friends were admiring the *branded dog paws*. Is that the new upgrade you and Bryce did?"

"Yes, Ma," I answered, hiding traces of complete shock.

I knew I saw them hovering around me in my delirium state.

Nathan Kilali

Of Papua New Guines, Enga

For his people; not his ego - Andarias Assh

All our lives are stories. Andarias Assh's story was one that the ignorant would say prideful, and the selfish would say egoistic. Even that is an understatement!
In memory of Late Andarias Assh:
(1920-2019)
My grandfather, my role model and my hero.

*Late **Andarias Assh** (left) with late **Kilali Mangus**, his co-grandfather at Wabag in 2010.*

Introduction

Andarias Assh (1920-2019), will be remembered as a generous old man, and a leader true to his word. For starters, I will refer to him as the good old man I last saw. I lived with him for half of my life. Throughout that time, I have witnessed all the good stories I heard about him, to be true. Even fascinating.

I was able to reason through why some of his actions and decisions were thought to be ruthless (as judged by some people) against his own family – 'it was for a greater cause!' Leaders are who they are because they know how to serve.

Heroes are not necessarily supernatural beings that we read in the comic books, or the Navy Seals that go to war. They are, but they can also be those who are dearest to us. More importantly, they are the ones who lay their lives down so others may live.

Andarias Assh, my grandfather, was a testament to both styles of leader, who I got to admire and look up to as my own hero. I learned and lived a part in his aging story. Even now after he's gone, his story continues to inspire.

On that note, it is a bitter truth, to my correct understanding, that Andarias Assh's story would need a three-hundred-page book for a greater audience. However, for the purposes of a short biography, it will be limited to **a few pages** like he used to do to his own stories when telling them to me.

And I hope as I write through these pages, his story, what he did for our country, would remain as **true** as he uttered it, and be read by many eyes and heard by many ears as it should be. In line with this, I choose not to rely on history books and articles to add details to the roles Andarias carried out in any of the chapters of Andarias' story. This would allow me to make assumptions on what Andarias might have done. Consequently, it would prompt me to write about things that Andarias did not do. This would be a disgrace and a dishonour to his good memory. Hence, I chose to be specific about what he actually did when he was carrying out those roles as I was told by Andarias himself, my mom and my relatives.

Background

Andarias Assh was born in 1920 at Yampu village in Kompiam-Ambum District, Enga Province. His mother had to cut his umbilical cord with a bamboo knife with his face down to the earth.

He grew up in those pre-independence days, when all the tales that we hear now were being lived by men. Such were the times when history was being made by the Westerners (white men) and off course, the indigenous people in Papua New Guinea.

Andarias was a typical native highlander. Growing up, his life revolved around tanget leaves, grass skirts, moka (compensation), tribal fights, traditional bride price ceremonies, sagai (a form of ritual), festivals including traditional dancing and ceremonies which mostly involved pigs and kina shells.

His father was a village leader as was his father before him. So, it was custom for Andarias to also be a leader in his village when he had reached adulthood. That was when he was in his mid-20s.

Andarias' education ended at Grade 6 at the Irelya Community School. Being taught by the white men at such a level at that time made him resourceful in many ways. He learnt new things, including Pidgin language (*Tok Pisin*) in which he eventually became really fluent.

Andarias, as an Interpreter

During the colonial period, the white men were advancing from the Coastal region into the Highlands. Unlike the Coastal areas, the people in the Highlands, especially in Enga Province, were fearsome warriors who were known for settling disputes through traditional tribal fights as part of their custom. They were hunters and gatherers who loved their land and bled for it.

The white men were coming into their land, not only as visitors but also to take it and develop it through western civilization. They came in with their own laws, motives and lifestyle which would surely have great impacts on the lives of the indigenous people.

Essentially, they were two different races with totally different ideologies, lifestyle, mindset, beliefs, and background. To bring them together and work to achieve the white men's objectives and to preserve the indigenous people's custom, good communication was needed.

In light of this, the white men decided to recruit natives who were fluent in Pidgin language as Interpreters. Andarias was also recruited when he was in his 20s. Andarias' style of interpretation was appealing to the white men. Also, the level of confidence, respect and influence he had over and from his people, became vital for there to be a smooth flow of communication between the landowners and the white men. This created understanding between these two groups and both groups' interests were served. In a way, the white men realised that Andarias' involvement was required for their expansion in that area.

A good illustration of this was during that time, the Kompiam Ambum road was about to be **built**. It was built not by huge machines and construction companies, but with the bare hands of the native landowners clamped on spades and crowbars.

Basically, Andarias helped the white men to carry out this massive construction. His role included, passing the white men's instructions to the natives on how to build the road.

After the road was built, certain developments were taking place in the Kompiam Ambum area. One of these is the Kompiam Court House. Andarias was promoted to be the lead interpreter in that Court house. He necessarily played the role of a Magistrate. Again, he played a significant role where he keenly wanted to see justice being served through the proper application of the laws of the white men and the custom of the indigenous people. This role was very vital because, in order for the court to make the right decisions, perfect communication was needed and Andarias never failed to achieve that. This court at Kompiam dealt with land issues, labour and law and order issues generally. Offenders were goaled.

Andarias' life as Luluai (Chief)

Official Luluais and tultuls were tribal and clan leaders who were appointed by the white men. Their main roles were to assist the Colonial Administration curb tribal fights and supervise construction of roads, airstrips, houses and other infrastructure in the area.

Andarias was promoted to be a Luluai after he had successfully served as a lead interpreter. This was during his 30s. He was given laplaps, a cap and a badge that he wore on his forehead. He mostly assisted the Australian Kiap (Patrol Official) to fast track control and the pacification of the Highland's tribes **(Bill, PNG Attitude, 2018)**.

He went to almost all parts of Kompiam Ambum District exercising the delegated power he was given to do administrative works of the white men. In these areas, Andarias was known for the beatings he gave to his fellow natives who did not listen to instructions or who had broken the law. Hence, the natives there were calm and obedient as ever in the eyes of the white men and Andarias.

One thing I learned after hearing these stories told by Andarias when he was a **Luluai** and an Interpreter, is standards – Andarias did the work he was delegated with pride and passion, and he was keen to see results.

It is evident from hereon that he spent the most part of his life travelling to and from Kompiam and Ambum Valley and he was too busy for a young man. He was selfless. He gave away most of his youthful and fruitful years, to do a better job to see change.

Andarias' relationship with the Missionaries

In the 1950s, the Divine Word Missionaries first came to that part of Enga. It was no surprise that Andarias was one of those native leaders that were first sought by the missionaries to work with them.

The Missionaries as commissioners of the Gospel were plain and were true to their agenda with no corrupt motives –

"They wanted the Gospel to reach as many people as possible". Andarias saw the need and importance of this. So as always, he was keen to help and show generosity to the Missionaries. He knew the best possible way to help: He gave away his land to the Divine Word Missionaries.

In 1952, Andarias and his good friend and clansman, **Saumb,** made the decision to give part of their land to the Missionaries. For two reasons: First, they were kind and generous. Second, they saw that the Missionaries were resourceful and were going to bring good changes for their people. In fact, the Missionaries did bring good changes.

The land that was given by Andarias and Saumb is where the Yampu Catholic Church and Yampu Health Centre (as part of Catholic Health Services) were built by the Divine Word Missionaries. These two community services have continued to serve the people of Enga and also PNG to this day.

Andarias not only did that. His good gestures continued when he influenced his other friends and clan leaders to be generous to the Missionaries too. This included his clansman, Saumb together with other clan leaders who had neighbouring lands at the upper part of Yampu village. They decided to give some of this piece of land to the Missionaries. This land is the size of two football fields. Today, the missionaries use this land to breed their live stocks and cattle.

Life in the Plantation

During the late 1950s, the Highlands Labour scheme was recruiting males to send them to work in different parts of

Papua and New Guinea. Luluais and tultuls did a useful job in recruiting these males. Andarias' outstanding role as a Luluai and also his ability to interpret was compelling to the white men that he was recruited to be one of those plantation labourers that were sent from Enga to work at the Rabaul Copra Plantation. He not only was a good labourer, but was also a good communicator in that part of the region. He was amongst the leaders of the Engans that went there.

Later, Andarias was promoted to be a **Bosboi** (Bossman) in the plantation. This was after he was married. He worked at the plantation for three years. Life at the plantation was really hard.

The Highlands labourers that went to the plantation were unskilled in this work. They were indentured (bonded) workers who were particularly exploited since the small-scale and scattered nature of copra plantation had the effect of pushing up costs and transportation costs and depressing wage levels to the absolute minimum. However, for these uneducated, unskilled men barely exposed to modernisation, it was the best thing to do to "earn" an income.

The sadder story is that most of these Highlanders did not return home as soon sooner as expected. The people back in the village thought of the worst things that could happen to them: the white men must have exiled and later killed them, or the coastal people must have killed them. Soon there were folk tales about these men and songs were sung by their loved one to honour their good memory.

Most the men returned home in the early 1980s. As for Andarias, he was lucky enough to return home after just three years. Though the reason for his early release was not mentioned to me by Andarias, I think it was like a reward given to him by the white men for the good job he did at the plantation.

Upon his **"release"**, he was given a bicycle and a torch with some shillings by the white men in consideration for his work as a Bossman in the plantation. I use the word **"release"** because life at the plantation was so harsh and the labourers had little to no freedom at all. The white men controlled and dictated what they wore, what they ate, when they slept and what time they started and finished work. Any misconduct in these areas was punished and they were goaled according to the *Native Labour Ordinance* that was regulating them. There was no room for rest, excuses or exercising of this and that right! It was non-existent.

As Keven Pamba recalls in a **National Newspaper Article (2018)** titled, *'Plantation Labourers: Our forgotten heroes'*, "these labourers made significant sacrifices to leave their homes (including their wives and children) to go away to places their ancestors never set foot to till the land. They literally put their bodies on the line in the searing heat of the tropics to build the young economy of PNG from their sweat, tears and blood. Yet the plantation labourers may never be accorded hero status nor will they be bestowed any honour – they are our forgotten national heroes."

Andarias' Married Life: An Engan man's love life

Andarias married my grandmother, Lusah Assh when he was reaching his 40s. Off course, their marriage and relationship was not one of those that we see today. It was more traditional. But one thing I always loved about their relationship is that, their love was a different kind. Living in this era I can say, it was more fairy tale-like. The words I will use to describe their relationship will surely reduce the solemnity of their relationship, and that is an injustice! Nevertheless, I urge the reader to take the genuine meaning of them all.

Lusah was Andarias' first ever lover and Andarias was Lusah's first love. They started having their love affair at their prime age and they did this for a long time. Their affair went on for many years until both Andarias and Lusah were ready for Marriage (i.e. customary marriage).

As both were strongly custom-oriented, it was immoral and disgraceful to have sex before marriage. It was strong custom that proper marriage through bride price payment must be paid to a girl for her to gain womanhood, and bring fame and wealth to her family. Hence, women in the Highlands respected their virginity and they greatly valued it.

The love that Andarias and Lusah had, knew no instant gratification. It involved processes of making stronger ties with the extended families and relatives, furnishing their character to be the right partner and getting the approval from parents. Their love was built through these processes over time. In a way, I can say they easily differentiated love from lust. So, Andarias and Lusah left no room for erotic or indecent thoughts to surface in their relationship.

This was nothing like what we see for today's lovers, which is breakable at any moment. Theirs was shielded by tender love, and respect. It was protected by their liberated custom. Principally, their patience and commitment throughout their relationship (before marriage) was not motivated by wealth, lust, pride, or greed. Their love was effortless and was a beautiful decider of their fate. Everything had to be the way it was in their relationship for us, (their children) to find good foundation in their marriage. We necessarily came to be a strong family and their memories echo loudly through all of us. If families break apart, this is what should bring them back together – "their ancestors' love".

One of the significant events that lead to their road to marriage was a ?? singsing singing festival. All the brides-to-be came together to sing and dance. When Lusah was delightfully dressed in her traditional attire - she was a beauty – Andarias asked Lusah's cousin to bring Lusah to Andarias' place so he could marry her. Lusah ran off with her cousin from the dancing ceremony to Andarias' home at Yampu. Henceforth, Andarias as a proud man married Lusah.

Andarias married Lusah in the late 1950s. This was when the Highlands Labour Scheme was underway, and the white men were recruiting natives. For Andarias and Lusah, this news was devastating: It was like being sent off to prison or being called to go to war. Plus, Andarias and Lusah had just married! Nonetheless, Andarias was going to go anyway, leaving his newly married wife behind.

Andarias' Descendants

When Andarias' work at the plantation ended, he came home to his wife at Yampu. Thereafter, in 1963, Andarias and Lusah had their first child, **Lena Kilali**, née Assh. Marriage and fatherhood were appealing to Andarias for him to stay back at the village for a while. So he took a break from his travels, and Andarias knew that break was going to be long. Andarias was looking forward to building his family back at home.

In 1965, Andarias' second child was born, **Daniel Assh**. In 1978, his third child was born, **Dii Assh**. Dii, for sure had the blessing of his old man and his mama; he went on to have five children that would make Andarias' geneology bigger.

In the late 1980s, Andarias had an affair with a woman called, Lapindawan. Lapindawan was a widow. She carried Andarias' fourth child, a girl, called **Esther Assh**. However, that affair only lasted two years. Lapindawan passed away leaving Esther behind. Lusah took Esther in and looked after her as her own daughter.

This affair with Lapindawan did not change the fact that Andarias loved Lusah. How could he forget about his long-time love, his old best friend, his soul mate that would live on with him to grow old and grey together, and one day pass through the next life together. Indeed, Andarias knew the difference between love and lust.

Lusah died on the 22nd of March, 2019, just a month after Andarias had passed on.

Andarias' Prayers

Andarias was a strong catholic. On Sundays, he went to the church that was built on his land. He was baptised together with his wife, Lusah. They made sure that all of their children were baptised by the catholic Father in the church as soon as they were of age.

When Andarias' was in his 80s, he became a relentless precant. He prayed every day for more than a decade until his last breath. I believe this was the most powerful of all the things he did. His prayers were selfless and pure. The prayers were a genuine thanksgiving for everything he had in life. Sadly, such prayers I hear no more.

Below is a daily morning prayer by Andarias in 2016, which I can recall from my fresh memory:

"Father, God. You have given us this new day as faithfully as You always do. The birds are singing Your praises. The skies stand still in awe of Your greatness. God, You are great and matchless to no man. You live in the Heavens above and I am on this earth. Yet, You have come to visit me in this earth, to have fellowship with me. I thank You for Your goodness and Your provisions. You have blessed me with long life. I thank You for the children and their families. Bless them and give them long life too. God, You are the God of this country, Papua New Guinea and You are watching over Papua New Guinea and protecting it. God You live in Papua New Guinea and I am realizing it to be true. God You are good and You are great. The whole earth must praise Your Name..."

Andarias would take longer periods to pray than the average person. He prayed three times a day: In the morning, at lunchtime, and during the night before sleeping. But that wasn't the only time he talked with God, he made daily conversations with Him about almost everything. He was a friend of God and he had an intimate relationship with Him.

Andarias' Last Moments: Living off Borrowed Time

The 21ˢᵗ century wasn't appealing to an old rock like Andarias from the early 20th century.

Nevertheless, he had his children and grandchildren to take care of his old skin through these borrowed times. My mom, **Lena**, gave birth to four children. The eldest son, Joel Kilali got married and the birth of his two children were celebrated by Andarias as a proud great-grand father. Gratefully, Andarias also got to live amongst us, his many great grandchildren, and we cherish the good memories and times we lived with him.

Andarias' life was indeed a blessing in disguise. He lived on to see all his grandsons and daughters, and even more interestingly give names to some of them. I can truly say that he lived a long life because of the relentless love and grace of God. He lived through the goodness of God.

Andarias first came to Port Moresby in 2013 with Lusah. In 2017, He and Lusah revisited Port Moresby to see the tall buildings, the city lights, the sea and its beach, and to feel the heat of the hot sun – "a fine experience for the two!" This was one of many treats by his son, **Dii** for Andarias to spend his borrowed time with his grandchildren. As such, his borrowed moments were never so grey.

Andarias' Departure

I think there is a different kind of death, and this is the one that the Creator orchestrated. But if He didn't, then I would claim this death as the most satisfying death that anyone could die.

Two weeks before his passing, Andarias knew that his journey was coming to an end. He told my Uncle that he wanted to leave Port Moresby, and go back to the village. It was one these moments I believe the land calls out to the souls of men. Still, it is a mystery that will never be solved. Even so, each person will unravel this mystery when their time comes.

Biblically, I think God was speaking to Andarias that his time was nearing. So he said to my Uncle, *"I have lived here enough, I have to go back home. I can't die in another man's land*

and give you that extra burden. You have looked after me well and I can't ask for more. I have to go back home to Yampu where my flesh belongs."

In **7ᵗʰ February, 2019,** on his dying bed, Andarias' last words were, *"My time has come and I'm going to a better place. You have all looked after me so well. My children, no harm will come to you. I leave you all in blessings and you shall all live well in this earth. Be with the Good Lord and he shall give you long life."*

Conclusion

Andarias dedicated his early days to do more than just good – "to bring change". He spent almost two decades being an interpreter, magistrate, a Luluai, and a labourer. He also helped the missionaries. He did his part in building the young economy of PNG. But he also found time to find love and get married. He found time to be a father, a grandfather and a great-grandfather. He also found time to be a leader back in the village. I think there is a balance in everything in life. I believe he found that balance. In our pursuit of life, I hope, we can find that balance too.

From what I've witnessed in my grandfather's life, I realized that we all have a birth date and a death date. In between that time frame, we all run a race. Some are more joyful; others are wretched from the start. It will all be a history, a sophisticated mystery for the knowledgeable.

Most of us will be forgotten throughout the long march of time. Nevertheless, we must not stop to do good deeds. Leaving some good memories and a legacy for later generations to appreciate seems like a nice thing to do. After all, it'll be a story to be read by many, and more beautiful will it be when it will be perfectly foretold by the **'One'** who orchestrated it.

To me the definition of a hero is generic – it may be our childhood marvel character, or the President of a country or those who have been in wars. But it can simply be someone close to us who was there when we needed him or her. As a kid, I needed someone to say, 'it's going to be alright'. We all need someone to tell us, 'you are loved', 'you are special and that you have a purpose.' The world is a cruel place to live and everybody in different moments in time need closure, protection, care, love and affection.

To my family or if not, to me, my grandfather was there for his people. His raw passion and selfless pride as a local Takikin man took him to secure a better future for his clan, his tribe and ultimately contribute his efforts to bring-forth civilisation towards that part of Kompiam and Ambum valley. That sounds more like a hero to me –

In honour of his loving Memory – Andarias Assh –

Thank you for your service, hero!

Acknowledgments

I have never written a biography before, especially one that would be out there for the world to read. None of this would be possible without my loving mom, **Lena Assh Kilali**. I thank her for sharing with me most of my grandfathers' life stories.

As she is the eldest child of Andarias Assh, she was the right person I could go to write this short biography of Andarias. Quite astonishing it was, when she perfectly remembered the dates chronologically, for each of the chapters of Andarias' life. It was effortless. Hence, I commend her for her great memory.

There was so much to write about but it was shortened to this. I wanted the story to be genuine, so I made sure that the information she gave me was true in all sense and unaltered. Hence, every time when she shared any stories of Andarias that I was familiar with, I would let her finish, and then later on, compliment her like: *"Wow, you do remember that correctly, mum. I knew that piece of information already but I was just testing you if you could remember it correctly too."* And then she would go on to say: *"Why would I lie about anything that Andarias did. It would be a disgrace and a dishonour to his loving memory."*

Special thanks to my two good friends, **Caleb Murian** and **Edwin Lyambi** who edited my work. When I reached out to them in the 11th hour and asked for their help, they weren't hesitant to give a hand.

I also thank my brother, **Joel Kilali** who sent me the photo of 'Andarias and Kilali'. I searched through all of my files for a photo of Andarias but I couldn't find any. Joel simply solved that problem for me.

First Nations Writers Festival, the team, the artists,
the workers, the stylists, the typesetters and all the wisdom
that flows from your experience and care.

It is all from you

That FNWF has come so far so quickly.

Thank you.

Bios

Euralia Paine, *Papua New Guinea*: Do cultures really clash? What is the norm in one culture? Aren't the ultimate goals the same in each? Is it the consequences of shifting lives that give rise to the clash, the problems? This intellectual challenge is presented by this author in her compelling story THE PROMISE.

Arnold Mundua, *Papua New Guinea*: Stories create the culture and the country; the history and the future. So that when you write a story – you literally write the country into being. A doyen of PNG literature, published for a long time, he is an Elder of Greater Pacific Literature. And his wonderful story has received an Award: AN UNEXPECTED INCIDENT AND I WAS MARRIED AGAIN. Just the title makes you happy.

Paulini Turagabeci, *Fiji*: The arc of a young woman's life, from the cultures of the past to the present....what? Beautifully narrated, structurally balanced, multi layered, almost light in nature – until you sit back at the end and think. This is magnificent literature from the Greater Pacific.

Baka Bina, *Papua New Guinea*: In a region of many languages [~ 1,000] culture is communication. FNWF intends to take these magnificent stories of the Greater #Pacific to the world. So this story uses three languages: Tok Ples, Tok Pisin, and English. Mr Bina's story KAUKAU BLUES could be used at home as well as around the world. A story of bartering for food highlights the counting used in the local language.

Lorna Saguba, *Papua New Guinea*: A poignant and beautiful story. Of young women moving along different life paths, which diverge from those secret whispered plans of their younger friendship. As those plans go awry, we all yearn for those plans of our youth. Or wonder what became of those old friends. Evocative of village life and life everywhere; generational customs; family; and young love.

Kogora Hale, *Papua New Guinea*: The Judges enthusiastically praised Mr Hale's story THE YELLOW BUTTERFLY as a charming depiction of life in PNG. Chance encounters, small moments matter, and we should hold and cherish them.

Marlene dee Gray Potoura, *Papua New Guinea*: Said "As a self-published author published all around the Pacific and internationally, I see the First Nations Writers Festival as the first and foremost organisation for all First Nation Writers to gather and share their culture through their stories. Listen up, we in the Greater Pacific have stories to tell. Join us please, I just love FNWF and the writers I have met [at FNWF2023] are exceptionally talented, and are working so hard to keep their indigenous stories alive. I tell you, winning a short story award this year with my piece, THE SINGING DOGS OF NEW GUINEA is unbelievable. I am still trying to let it all sink in." Thank you for joining us, Ms dee Gray Potoura. A renowned Elder of the Greater Pacific literary community.

Nathan Kilali, *ENGA* Papua New Guines: A memoir FOR HIS PEOPLE NOT HIS EGO – ANDARIAS ASSH (1920-2019). A warm story of 100 years from the first colonisers to old age. As told to and remembered by his grandson; with love: My grandfather, my role model and my hero.

From First Nations Writers Festival 2022 — the inaugural book award winner Joshua Torenn of the Solomon Islands brings a landmark narrative of fiction. Rich with ancient cultural knowledge and empathy, contemporary clashes, fast paced, and visceral. This heartbreaking story is about ethnic and economic disruption; greed; and families striving forward. Only someone imbued with a millennia of knowledge could write it.

THE
BANDITS
AMONGST
US

A THRILLER

JOSHUA TORENN
SOLOMON ISLANDS

The first full length novel in 40 years to be published by a Solomon Islander.

"Bernard Maneboko, was born in a village in rural Guadalcanal, Solomon Islands. He had a bright future, attended a prestigious school, and had dreams of becoming a Police Officer.

But his dreams were disrupted on the cold December night in 1999, when the brigands broke into his family's home and burnt it to the ground. An ethnic crisis erupted on the Island of Guadalcanal.

Both parents gone and as the only child and survivor, he had to face life on his own. But that is not all, a logging company is heading for his village, without his tribe's consent.

Teamed up with his peers, the BANDITS, he must fight the logging-mongers. In doing so, he dices with death -- facing the ferocious mountain rebels, trading with the crooked Chinese merchants and eventually pleading his case with the Police.

In his search for answers, he exposes an horrific past, which positions him as the next potential target in the series of murders. Bernard must get to the root of it to stop the brutal killings."

A FNWF2023 Award Winner - the Judges said of this book John W Kuri enlivened the ancient myths, fantasy and sorcery of the Greater Pacific to transcend tribal boundaries.

These cultural foundations of tradition, culture and belief systems were created by First Nations peoples all around the world. Judges were "enchanted and horrified in turn, as the memories of youth were re-imagined in these ancient ethereal characters. This book evokes ancient myths and sorcery of the type found in the acclaimed and award winning Indigenous Australian "Cleverman" television fantasy series and the recent multi award winner "Prey" replete with Comanche Native American customs and culture". John Kuri was born to Simbu parents, he now works and lives in Port Moresby, Papua New Guinea. Educated in the Simbu province and the Eastern Highlands, he studied Science at the University of Papua New Guinea.

In this second book in the Porugl Trilogy, Porugl has returned to Gandia from the Underworld. This is unheard of and his return sparks joy amongst the people. He learns his father has been murdered in his absence. However, he wishes to start a normal life in Gandia with Maie, a beautiful young woman. He assimilates back into village life, passes his initiation and along the way meets Waine, who crafts an everlasting bow for him. But the Underworld is not done with him yet. Kerwanba's pride has been shattered. She will do anything to end Porugl's life. She sends her minions out to see if there is any man in Kondaland brave enough to carry out her wishes. But there is no man just a certain young woman. Everything begins to work out for Kerwanba and the whole of Gandia village is destroyed. Kerwanba releases her most secret weapon yet.